BREEZY FRIENDS AND BODIES

A RAINA SUN MYSTERY

ANNE R. TAN

To Khai,
for giving me the space to write

1

———

A SYMBIOTIC RELATIONSHIP

Raina jerked her head from the pages of the journal when the back door opened and the laughter and hubbub of conversations drifted out from the house. After a quick glance over her shoulder, she ducked underneath the staircase in the backyard. She clutched her deceased grandfather's journal to her chest and hoped Uncle Martin would go back inside when he saw the empty yard.

She turned off the light on her cell phone and slipped it into her pocket. She'd waited two years to find this treasure, so a few more minutes would be a breeze. The damp fog rolling in from the San Francisco Bay made the recent injury on her knee ache.

The wind shifted, and acrid smoke and snippets of Uncle Martin's conversation drifted downwards. "...New Year's Eve dinner...liver...humane." The discussion with the butcher became more technical and Raina's attention drifted off.

Sometimes Chinese New Year could be just as

annoying as Christmas with everyone wanting to appear outwardly benevolent. Who cared how the cow was slaughtered? Dead was dead. Absolution shouldn't come in the form of loose change clanging against the collection box during holidays or how a cow was treated at his death.

Footsteps came down the stairs, drowning out the rest of the conversation. Dust showered on Raina with each thudding step. She blinked rapidly, trying to clear the grit from her eyes. She felt like a naughty child instead of the grown woman she was, but a retiree with too much free time was the worst kind of busybody.

The last thing she needed going into Chinese New Year were uncomfortable questions about Ah Gong's secret family in China. As if she knew why or how her grandfather was able to keep this skeleton for fifty years. At the moment, she wanted to know how his journal ended up in her older sister's house.

Raina shifted her cold bottom, but it only increased the pins and needles sensation. Geez, why didn't the man get on with it? He must be sitting on the steps, just on the other side of where she huddled. She could imagine the cigarette dangling from his mouth and bobbing in time to his words.

Her eyes had adjusted to the darkness, and she saw the outline of the lawn furniture stacked in one corner with plastic covers over them. What she wouldn't give to pull one of the chairs out.

Chinese superstition held that anything a person did during this critical period prior to the celebration for the New Year was an omen of things to come. If this superstition were true, then Raina had a year of skulking in cold, dark places to look forward to. Wonderful.

Another minute ticked by. Uncle Martin shifted, and dust rained down between the cracks again. Raina covered her mouth with one hand to muffle her sneeze. The silence stretched on. This was ridiculous. Were they trying to out wait each other?

She waited a few more minutes and crawled out from underneath the staircase—only to find Uncle Martin looking straight at her with an expectant smile. The single naked bulb at the stoop did little to illuminate the foot of the stairs. His face was half hidden by shadows. Throw in the swirling fog and cloying cigarette smoke, and this could be a spooky encounter if Raina hadn't known the seventy-year-old man her entire life.

Uncle Martin wasn't technically an uncle. He was married to her grandmother's cousin at one point, but they were divorced by the time Raina was born. Strangely, it was the cousin who disappeared from their lives and the ex-husband that hung around the family.

"I thought you were behind the apple tree," Uncle Martin said.

Raina hugged the journal across her chest as if the flimsy book were a shield. The hair on the back of her neck stood at attention. It sounded as if Uncle Martin was aware of her nefarious activity and sought her out.

"Should I be concerned we have another ninja in the family?" he asked, the laughter in his voice grating on her nerves.

"No, I wouldn't think of intruding on Po Po's fantasy." Her grandma was notorious for her inventive costumes.

He chuckled. "What do you have there? That looks

like one of your grandfather's old journals. I don't understand why people want to record what happens in their lives."

She gave him a noncommittal tight smile, the kind one gave to a talkative passenger on a bus to discourage further conversation without being outright rude. "I better go back upstairs. It's almost time for Lila to open presents."

"Where's your Po Po? I'm surprised she's not at her great-granddaughter's birthday party."

He flicked the cigarette butt into the darkened yard and slipped a new one in his mouth, his lips tightening around the cylinder. His hand screened the wind while the other hand clicked on the lighter.

She plucked the lighter from his hands and slipped it into her pocket. "One is plenty, Uncle Martin."

He slipped the cigarette back into the pocket of his sweater. "You're starting to act like your grandma."

Raina smiled. There was no better compliment. "Po Po should be back for the New Year's Eve dinner. Her best friend had an outpatient procedure."

Bonnie Wong, or Po Po as Raina had always called her maternal grandmother, was popular among the local retirees and ate marriage proposals for breakfast. There weren't too many seventy-five-year-olds with her energy or full set of teeth.

"Raina, I need your help. When is Bonnie coming back to San Francisco?" Uncle Martin asked again.

"I just told you. Po Po will be back before the end of the week."

Uncle Martin tugged at the collar of his sweater, the wobbly loose skin on his throat spilling over the fabric.

"Oh, right." He took a deep breath. "I need you to convince your grandma to go out on a date with me."

Raina's eyes widened until she felt like a bug-eyed toad. She'd never been asked to play matchmaker before. If it were up to her, she would run a background check on each and every suitor. "How come you don't ask her yourself?" she asked, stalling for time. Her grandma would never forgive Raina for her interference. "You, of all people, should know she is perfectly capable of making her own decisions."

"Bonnie didn't like the idea." Uncle Martin frowned, staring over Raina's shoulder as if remembering past rejections. "Look, she trusts you. You're the only one she asked to clear out her husband's stuff. You can convince her."

His faith in her influence stood on quicksand. Things had been rocky between Raina and her grandmother since their Christmas blow-up on the interpretation of lying.

He didn't need to know cleaning out the attic was Po Po's passive-aggressive punishment because Raina "lied by omission." How was she to know her promise to her dying grandfather would lead to the role of confessor for his infidelity? Then again, maybe Raina misunderstood the entire thing. After all, she wasn't a mind reader.

"I am Switzerland. Totally neutral when it comes to my grandmother's love life," Raina said. Rumor had it Uncle Martin had money of his own, but he didn't have the vigor to match her grandma nor did he have the calming personality that could temper Po Po's razzle-dazzle. "She doesn't comment on the men I date and I extend the same courtesy to her."

"Fate can be such a shyster. I had to fall in love with the woman who was engaged to my best friend." His mouth twisted into a grimace. "I cared for my ex-wife. And I tried to make our marriage work, but sometimes you only fall in love once in a lifetime and everyone else pales by comparison."

Raina's eyes softened. Was this the reason Uncle Martin stayed close to the Wong family all these years? How come she never felt like this about anyone? Well, she did have a passion like this once, but Matthew didn't want her. "I don't know..."

"It's now or never. I can't spend the rest of my life waiting. My liver is failing. Who knows how many years I have left? And with what time I do have, I want to show your grandma a good time."

Raina gave him a sideways glance. Yuck! There wasn't enough bleach in the world to scrub away the image of Uncle Martin doing the Hokey Pokey with Po Po.

"Just put in a good word for me. Get Bonnie and me in the same room. I will take it from there. Please, Raina, I could make your grandma happy," Uncle Martin said, the words tumbling out now that he got over the difficult part.

Raina shook her head. No way was she getting involved. If she kept another secret from her grandma, it would be the end of their relationship. The truth always had a way of coming out.

"What can I do to get you to help me?" Uncle Martin asked.

"Sorry, there's nothing I need so desperately that would make me want to interfere with my grandma's love life."

"I can tell you the truth about what happened in China in nineteen sixty-two." He nodded at the journal in Raina's hands. "Stuff that might not be in there."

Raina froze, turning her head like a puppet to stare at the elderly man who had been a benign uncle to her until this evening. Her deceased grandfather had acquired a secret family in nineteen sixty-two. At his death, he had left three million dollars in Raina's custody for their upkeep. This secret had dictated her life for two years.

"What do you know?" she said through numb lips.

He wagged his index finger. "Na-ah. Not until you get me a date with Bonnie."

Before Raina could continue her conversation, the back door clicked opened. Her sister, Cassie, peered out into the backyard. "There you are, Rainy. It's time for the birthday cake."

Uncle Martin got up, brushing the dirt off his pants. "Just think about it. This could be the beginning of a symbiotic relationship." He chuckled as if he made a world-class joke.

RAINA SLID a sideways glance at a laughing Uncle Martin by the grouping on her right. Next to him stood a tall distinguished man with a round gut that would make a potbelly pig jealous. Mom sailed in from the kitchen with a platter of goodies and the men immediately shifted to welcome her into the group.

All the designer furniture was pushed up against the walls, leaving a clear space in the middle of the great room. The younger children had been relegated to the den with the nanny hours ago. As the brigade of wine and beer exchanged hands, everyone spoke over the person next to them, so the room clamored like a broken bell. This was turning out to be some two-year-old birthday party.

Cassie snapped her fingers in front of Raina's face to get her attention. "What are you looking at?" She turned around, and her sleek black hair fanned out behind her. The lights bounced off the gloss like liquid mercury. Raina would willingly give up a molar for a mane like that.

Mr. Potbelly reached over and squeezed their mother's waist. Mom's favorite dating advice to her daughters comprised of pumping men up with food to ensure they didn't stray too far from home, which never made sense since their dad had been a health nut. Apparently she'd found someone who didn't mind being pumped.

"Who is the man with Mom?" Raina asked.

"Do you remember Hudson Rice, Uncle Martin's nephew? He moved back from L.A. last year to take over the family business. It was the only way Uncle Martin could retire," Cassie said.

Raina did a double take, trying to reconcile the overweight man with the fit playboy in her memory. The thinning black hair held more streaks of gray. Time had blurred much of the Eurasian features, but the ice blue eyes still flashed with a wry humor she remembered from her childhood.

Cassie smirked. "He didn't age well, huh? I heard it's from partying too much."

"Nobody really ages well. I'm surprised Hudson has

gained so much weight. He used to be a marathon runner." Was this Raina's future staring at her? Maybe she should add weights to her routine. Rail-thin with a head of curly black hair like a dandelion puff, she didn't need a daily run, but without the endorphins, she couldn't guarantee her family's safety within spitting distance.

Cassie's mouth tightened as if she took personal offense. Their relationship was touch and go ever since Raina had refused to pay off her sister's credit cards last year. "I'm aging well and so is Mom."

Raina averted her gaze, glancing down at the wineglass in her hands. At thirty, of course her sister was "aging well" compared to someone in his late forties. And their mother was a socialite, flitting around the City like a butterfly. This kind of living sure could age someone. "Is Mom dating him?"

"I hope so. He's Uncle Martin's heir. And besides, how cool is it that Mom is dating a younger man?"

Raina glanced at Hudson again. Just because he would inherit the family business didn't mean he was financially solvent, especially since his living depended on Chinese faith and superstition. "I'm surprised Mom has taken up with a reformed player."

"I think it's cool she gets to tame the bad boy."

Raina raised an eyebrow. How bad could Hudson Rice be when he couldn't even see his toes?

Cassie continued, "Changing topics. Why did Po Po want you to clear out Ah Gong's stuff from the house? "

Raina licked her lips. She had to tread carefully so her sister wouldn't stalk off in a huff before she had time to ask about the journal. "I don't think Po Po can handle going through his stuff. Even though he has been dead for two years, it's painful to close the door on fifty years of marriage." More so when he was a cheating rat. "If you're feeling left out, you're more than welcome to come help me."

"Is she planning to sell the Victorian? Why did she buy a condo in Gold Springs?"

"I don't know."

"Come on, you must know something. She moved into the dinky little town you call home. I don't understand why anyone would want to leave the City."

"I really don't know," Raina said, trying to keep the irritation out of her voice. Gold Springs wasn't dinky. "Po Po is a grown woman. Why would I question what she does?"

"I can't afford to have Mom and Win move in with us. It's not fair for grandma to sell the house from underneath them. Why don't you buy the house for Mom with the money Ah Gong left you? It'll be the perfect solution for your ill-gotten gains."

Raina took a deep breath to keep from exploding. Why did everyone assume she had done something underhanded because she inherited three million dollars while all the grandchildren had gotten one dollar each, including her sister? "It's Po Po's house. She can do whatever she wants with it. A Victorian with a garage in Pacific Heights costs over three million dollars."

"Po Po can give you a discount. You wouldn't be so laissez-faire if you were still living in the family home."

"Which is kind of the point. Mom is in her fifties and she never held a job. She ignores all her responsibilities, and we both know she's more of a teen than our brother.

Don't you find shopping and lunch dates to be a frivolous existence?"

Cassie stiffened. "What is that supposed to mean?"

Raina groaned inwardly. Talk about open mouth and insert foot. Her sister had followed in their mom's footsteps—marrying right out of college to an older man, forgoing the chance at a career to be a housewife.

"Nothing. That's what I'll end up with at the rate I'm going. No career. No husband. No house. No kids."

"Oh, honey." Cassie was all smiles now. "Can't you get another engineering job? You don't need a man if you can support yourself."

Raina suppressed her snort at the irony. "I like grad school, and I still have hopes of being Indiana Jones someday."

"He was an archaeologist. Even I know there's a difference between an archaeology and history degree."

Raina ignored the barb. So what if she wasn't a particularly enthusiastic grad student, but the college provided full health benefits which she couldn't afford otherwise. "Talking about history"—she pulled the battered book from her back pocket—"this journal documents Ah Gong's time in China during the Great Leap Forward." The gold leaf-embossed Chinese character for longevity on the cover gleamed in the light.

"Where did you find it?"

"Taped behind the vanity mirror in the master's bathroom."

Her sister raised an eyebrow. "What were you doing in my bedroom?"

"The hall bathroom had a line. I didn't think you would want me to pee on your carpet." Raina shook the journal to re-focus their conversation. "Do you have any idea how this got there? Can I keep this?"

"I don't see why you're so excited. You probably don't even know anyone he mentions in it. And no, I have no idea how it got in my bedroom."

Raina slipped the journal back into her pocket. She was used to her sister's lack of interest in anything outside her restrictive world. "This is history. Our history."

"If you say so." Cassie looked over Raina's shoulder, stretching out her hands. "Come to Mommy."

Raina turned to see her brother-in-law approaching with her niece. Mom and her friends watched the birthday girl with beaming smiles.

Lila clapped her hands and leapt out of her dad's arms. "New Rain. New Rain."

Raina caught the two-year-old before she could tumble to the ground. Her niece always called her by the literal translation of her Chinese name. Lila wiggled in her arms.

"Careful, Raina." Cassie held out her hands. "Come to Mommy, sweetie."

Lila ducked her head and clung to her aunt.

"Why don't you visit with the rest of the family? I can watch her," Raina said, hoping to soften the blow. It wasn't her fault her stay-at-home sister needed a nanny to watch her only child.

Cassie opened her mouth to argue, but before she could say anything, Blue appeared. He leaned in and kissed Raina on the top of her head.

Raina supposed Blue, whose real name was Sebastian Luc, was her boyfriend. Her uncle had introduced them two months ago. He was also a good friend of Cassie's husband, which was strange since Benson usually didn't have time for someone who didn't help him get ahead.

"Today is my lucky day. I get to have three beautiful ladies all to myself," Blue said.

Cassie rolled her eyes.

Blue tickled the child's chin. "And what kind of birthday cake did you get, little pony?"

Lila let out a loud neigh, causing other people in the room to look in their direction. The child ducked her head onto her aunt's shoulder at the unexpected attention. Raina rubbed her small back, smiling.

Blue laughed. "I see someone has been practicing."

"Now, Lila, we need to use our words," Cassie said. "You shouldn't be encouraging her." She grabbed Lila and stalked over to join their mom.

The smile slipped off Raina's face. So much for their sisterly relationship. Rocky would be a nice way to describe it, but arctic might be more accurate. She swallowed the lump in her throat. Her life was fine without her big sister's approval.

2

______

A FRENCH K-I-S-S

After Lila opened her gift, Raina drifted away from the crowd to gather her purse and jacket from the hall closet. Her head pounded and her shoulders were tight. Being around her large extended family was normally stressful enough, but now that she was also the black sheep, she would rather have kidney stones. At least with the medical condition she would have an excuse to get snappish instead of biting her tongue at every other conversation. But the squeal from Lila when she opened Raina's gift had made it all worth it.

"Taking off already? Can I give you a ride home?" Blue said from behind her. "I don't really want to stay without you."

Raina spun around. "No, thank you. I'm sorry. I didn't want to interrupt your conversation with Benson." She clutched the jacket in front of her, much to her chagrin at being caught sneaking off rather than leaving him behind. Her boyfriend had been her brother-in-law's friend long before they started dating.

His gold-flecked eyes searched hers, softening at whatever he found. He pulled her close for a hug, resting his chin on the top of her head. "I'll walk out with you. I'm done here, too."

Raina's body melted at his touch. She closed her eyes to breathe in the male scent—an odd mix of Downy laundry detergent and sawdust. His large hands rubbed her shoulders until the tension disappeared.

"Call or text me when you get home so I know you're safe," Blue whispered.

Raina pulled back to study his face. No argument about how dangerous it was for a woman to walk around in the dark by herself? Her last boyfriend would have argued with her until the sun came up, and then flung her on his shoulder to make sure she got home safe.

She leaned forward and gave him a kiss on his cheek. "Good night," she whispered. Should they move to the next level or make a clean break? They enjoyed each other's company, but living two hundred miles apart complicated things. And moving back to San Francisco wasn't on her radar.

They left the house together and parted ways. The short walk was cold and foggy, and after a year of living in Gold Springs, she was no longer used to the bay area weather. By the time she entered the BART station, Raina regretted declining the ride. She knew all about lying in beds she made, which included frozen toes at the moment and being the black sheep.

The platform for the BART station was crowded. A

school of sardines had more breathing room. No one made eye contact, preferring to stare at their noses or their phones. Who knew what crazies one would attract by showing a flash of humanity?

Raina inched forward until she stood in front of the painted yellow square on the floor, indicating where the train doors would slide open upon arrival. While the doors had never closed on her, she secretly feared they would, just like the elevator when one was half a second too slow.

She bounced on the balls of her feet for something to do. The journal tucked in her purse burned her imagination. She wanted nothing more than to whip it out to devour the pages. But one didn't tune out in a crowded subway station.

The bright headlights of the approaching train could be seen in the dark tunnel. The noise increased on the platform—the train rattling the rail, passengers gathering their belongings, and the air vibrating as it was pushed forward by pounds of speeding steel.

The strap of Raina's purse jumped on her shoulder. She snatched at it instinctively and turned to see someone yanking at it from behind her. The tug-of-war lasted half a heartbeat, and the mugger jerked the strap out of her hands, leaving her palms stinging. As he turned away from her, his sharp elbow rammed into her side, bumping her off balance.

Raina stumbled backwards and her hands grasped air. She fell onto the train tracks, the impact knocking the breath out of her, and she lay on the rail—stunned.

The mugger must have heard her distress. He paused

in his escape to stare at her and his mouth opened, causing the scar on the edge to grow longer. Whatever he said was lost in the hubbub. As if from the end of a long tube, Raina caught a muffled "sorry." The crowd closed in and he disappeared from view.

The rail vibrated against her back. As Raina scrambled to her feet, a wave of dizziness washed over her and she swayed. She bit her tongue and focused on the pain. She could play the swooning princess once she got out of here.

A woman on the platform screamed, pointing at the approaching train in the tunnel. What a genius.

A man in a pinstripe suit dropped to his stomach on the platform, reaching for her. "Grab my hands."

Raina's fingers brushed the man's outstretched hands. She jumped, and he grabbed onto her hands. Her legs scrabbled against the vertical wall, moving up inches at a time.

Time slowed, and everything sharpened as if her brain decided to take a snapshot. There was the pinstripe man's cologne, a woodsy scent with a hint of mint, and the damp on her hands—she didn't know if it came from her or the man—and the chill of the air rushing toward them.

"The train is coming." The woman fanned her flushed face. "Oh, I feel faint."

Another man grabbed the woman and moved her away from the edge of the platform. She collapsed onto her fellow passengers like she was the star of a show.

The woman sat up and pointed. "What is he doing? He'll get killed!"

The squeal of brakes on metal grated like the screaming woman's high-pitched voice. Another man reached across the pinstripes man to grab Raina's armpits. Both men heaved and, for a split second, Raina hung in the air, then bellyflopped onto the platform.

Cold air rushed past her. The train glided to a stop six inches from where she lay. She could kiss the dirty floor with the blackened bubblegum patches...once she stopped wanting to throw up.

AFTER THANKING the pinstripes man profusely, Raina waved off the need to call for an EMT. While the medical technicians would be welcomed, the ambulance bill would give her heartburn months later. There wasn't much an EMT could do for her bruises that she couldn't do herself. Nope—ice and Tylenol had worked well enough in the past.

It took another hour and a half to answer questions from the BART police and SFPD about the mugging. They promised to call if they recovered her purse or nabbed the mugger, but Raina wasn't holding her breath.

Raina called her brother for a ride, and Win showed up in twenty minutes. She followed him to his car, the adrenaline from playing chicken with the train rushed out of her. A deflated balloon probably had more air than she did, but she still had to hold it together until she could crawl into bed.

The fog swirled around them, dimming the street-lights and reducing visibility to only a few feet. Whoever thought the thick clouds were romantic hadn't walked in the damp chill in the middle of the night, bone-weary with an ache on the backside. Win drove completely focused on the road.

Why did she put up a fight? It was a cheap purse. Her grandfather's journal was the only thing of value. She swallowed the lump in her throat. Nothing she could do about it at the moment.

Raina must have dozed off because the next thing she knew, Win was nudging her awake. The windows were dark, so Mom hadn't left the party yet.

"Sorry for making you leave early," she mumbled, unbuckling her seat belt.

"Are you going to tell me what happened?" her seventeen-year-old brother asked, concern written all over his face.

"Nope. It's no big deal."

"Your jeans are filthy, your jacket sleeve is torn, and you're walking with a limp. I say it's a big deal."

Raina focused on keeping her voice steady. "Don't worry about it. I'm okay." She got out of the car, not wishing to continue the conversation.

Win opened the front door for her, and they went inside. She was on her way to the guest room when her brother called out.

"Rainy, he...he didn't rape you, did he?" His voice squeaked in the end, reminding her how young he was.

The gears shifted through the molasses in her brain, and it took Raina a heartbeat to process what her brother was asking. "No, it's not like that. I got mugged." She blinked rapidly but wasn't able to stop the tears.

Win enclosed her in a warm embrace. "Shh...it's okay. You're home now."

Raina tried to stop, but soon his sweater dampened beneath her cheek. In what felt like hours later, she regained a semblance of control. She pushed away from him. "Don't tell Mom. I don't want her to freak out."

"How did you get mugged? Wasn't Blue with you?"

"No, I didn't want him to drive across town to drop me off. He has to work tomorrow, and his day starts at five in the morning," Raina said, filling in the story so Blue didn't look as if he ditched her when it was she who wanted to get rid of him.

Win's mouth tightened. "Well, that's a boyfriend's job. If he can't see you home, he shouldn't be taking you out in the first place."

"Winter Theodore Sun, when did you become my dad?"

"When he told me I was the man of the house at seven. Good night, sis."

As her baby brother headed up the stairs, Raina blinked at another round of tears threatening to spill out. Win had been seven when their dad died of cancer.

RAINA PEELED BACK her eyelids with a groan. The digital display on the alarm clock in the guest room said it was five after seven. She stumbled out of bed and into the hall to grab the ringing phone on the narrow table. "Hello?"

"This is Mom. How come you're not picking up your cell?"

"Dead battery," Raina lied. She'd almost forgotten about the mugging incident.

"Is Po Po coming home today? I promised to pick up her favorite dan tat from the Golden Gate Bakery, but I'm busy this morning."

Raina closed her eyes against the weak light coming in from the window. She didn't want to talk about her grandma's favorite egg tart. "Mom? Are you calling me from your room?"

Silence.

She glanced at her mother's bedroom door. "I'm coming in."

"I'm not home right now. Hudson and I are having breakfast."

Mom's new boyfriend must be something else to get her out of the house before eleven o'clock. "Can't you get the dan tats afterward?"

"I'm clear across town. Can you do this teensy little favor for your mom? This will give you a break from hauling those dusty boxes out of the attic."

Raina grunted. Some break. It would take her longer to drive the three miles than it did to make dinner. Public transportation wasn't that much faster. Was the Golden Gate Bakery the one with the line out the door that wrapped around the corner? Or was that the Golden Dragon Bakery?

"You're a gem, hon. You saved me two hours."

Raina hung up and got ready for the day. Now wasn't the time to examine her mommy issues. She was here to help her grandma clean out her grandfather's things so Po Po could start the Year of the Monkey off right. Any other family issues would have to take a number.

At first, she had thought the sudden appearance of her grandfather's journal was a sign to reveal his secret to the rest of the family. She'd carried the burden on her own long enough. But now, she didn't know what to think. If only the mugger had picked another mark.

It took two and a half hours to finish her errands. With Mom's car in the garage and a driveway too short to fit another, Raina ended up parking two blocks away from the house and making three trips to bring the groceries in. Then she unloaded the food. Not only did the county-wide ban on plastic bags mean toting reusable bags before any shopping expedition, it also meant inspecting them to make sure they were clean afterward.

Of course, Mom wasn't home to help. Little things like keeping her family fed were beyond her limited abilities. Raina knew she was wasting too much emotional energy on a situation she couldn't change. Unlike her brother, she had her cozy apartment in Gold Springs. In the meantime, she'd just have to get through the next few days.

The doorbell rang as Raina folded the last of the reusable shopping bags. She hurried to the front door and peered through the peephole. A man in a bicycle helmet held a clipboard. His messenger bag bulged with packages and letters.

She opened the door. "Can I help you?"

The courier glanced at his clipboard. "Raina Sun?"

Her eyes widened. Was she being served? Who did she piss off recently? "I am she."

He pointed to a blank spot on the form. "Sign here, please."

She signed and was rewarded with a small cardboard box. "Who is this from?"

The courier bounced down the stairs and unlocked his bike. "Check the return address," he called over his shoulder and took off.

Raina glanced at the smudged return address. She couldn't make out anything other than it was from someone in the city. A sense of déjà vu settled over her and her stomach flipped with unease. The last time she'd encountered a package from an unknown sender, it had exploded, covering her from head to toe in pink slime.

She closed the door and returned to the kitchen, gingerly placing the package on the island. The lucky cat clock ticked, its little plastic eyes and tail swaying back and forth to the seconds. She took a deep breath. This was not a repeat of the last time. No one was trying to curse her. With a package knife in her hand, she reached for the box.

The phone rang. A loud piercing *cha-ling-a-ling*.

Raina jumped and dropped the knife. She abandoned the task and picked up the phone. "Hello?"

All she got was a dial tone. If this was a B-rated horror movie, she was determined not to end up playing the dead bimbo. She returned the phone to the cradle. The silence in the kitchen was deafening. No creaking floorboards. No TV in the background. Her stomach churned at the realization that she was in the old Victorian by herself.

Cha-ling-a-ling. Cha-ling-a-ling.

Raina snatched the phone. "Hello," she barked into the receiver. "Hello."

No answer.

It had to be one of the teenage girls who had a crush on her younger brother prank calling. Her hands shook when she returned the phone to the cradle.

BAM! BAM!

Raina swiveled her head, glancing at the hallway that led to the front door. The doorknob rattled. Someone was determined to get into the house.

3

A SMALL PRANK

As Raina peered through the privacy glass cutout in the front door, her heart hammered in her chest. She could make out blurred red shapes on the landing and nothing else. Did the courier return with another package? Did she really want to see what was on the other side of the door?

BAM!

A loud knock came from the backdoor in the kitchen.

Raina jumped as if someone prodded her with a hot iron. Her fingers curled into fists. Enough already. She wasn't going to let a prankster terrify her in her childhood home.

As Raina jerked the door open, she yelled, "What do you want?"

There was no one on the landing.

The pink bakery box from the Golden Gate Bakery rested on top of a red suitcase. She leaned out, glancing up and down the street. What was her grandma's luggage doing at the house?

"What are you doing?" Po Po asked from behind her.

Raina stumbled over the threshold, banging her funny bone against the doorframe. The tingly sensation ran the length of her arm.

Her grandma peered at her above fake half-moon glasses. "Rainy, you can't even put on underwear without hurting yourself. I'm surprised you're able to walk around without a helmet."

Raina shook her arm, hoping to dull the pain. "How did you get inside the house? I thought you would be in Gold Springs for a few more days."

"I came in through the back door using the doghouse key. How come you didn't answer my calls or open the front?" Po Po asked, sounding miffed at having to come in from the back door. There was a backdoor key hidden in the doghouse in the backyard.

"I did, but you hung up both times when I picked up," Raina said, just as put off herself. "Where are your keys?"

Po Po shrugged, reaching for the bakery box. "It's somewhere in the condo. I hightailed out of town this morning as soon as Matthew showed up. Maggie is cranky from cabin fever. I told him to load his grandma up with can soup and said I would be back in a few days to check on her. If I'd known Matthew would be back so soon, I would have come home last night for Lila's party."

Raina went into the house, dragging the suitcase inside and setting it next to the stairs. She pretended the news of her ex-boyfriend's activities was no more inter-esting than a discussion about the weather. She followed her grandma into the kitchen.

Po Po cocked her head and studied Raina. "You're too

quiet. What's going on? Why are you...nervous?" Her grandma's tone became serious.

"Nothing."

"I can tell by your voice. Did you get a spook? The ghost will leave you alone if you leave out a burning incense." Po Po mumbled to herself. "Geez, why doesn't anyone listen to me?"

"No, it has nothing to do with her." The ghost her grandma was referring to was "Weeping May," a Chinese lady who threw herself off the balcony in the 1920s when she was jilted at the altar. No one in the family had encountered her, except for Po Po. "I got a package from an unknown sender a minute ago."

"What's in it?"

"I was just about to open it."

"Uh-huh. Are your underpants smoking yet? I bet you were looking for an excuse to delay opening it."

Raina glanced at the cardboard box. Her grandma was right. She reached for the package knife and from the corners of her eyes noticed Po Po taking a step back. She sliced the package and opened the flaps.

Nestled among Styrofoam peanuts was her purse.

Her hands shook as she laid the packaging knife on the kitchen island. Why would someone mug her and return her purse? Either the mugger knew her, or whoever he worked for did. And this person knew her well enough to know where she stayed when she was in the City since her driver's license showed her Gold Springs home address.

"Rainy?" Po Po sounded concerned.

"It's my purse." Raina explained the whole story,

starting with finding the missing journal and the mugging at the BART station a few hours later.

Po Po's posture stiffened at the mention of her husband's journal. "Did you read it?" she whispered.

"I could only verify it belonged to Ah Gong before I got roped into a chat with Uncle Martin."

"Is there anything missing from the purse?"

Raina reached for the box and paused. "Should I be concerned about fingerprints?" Fear was making her careless. The mugger would have wiped the bag down before mailing it back to her.

Po Po snorted in disgust. "Really?"

Raina inventoried the items. Cell phone, wallet, keys, lip balm, hair tie, a pen, and...a package of firecrackers? "The journal is missing, and the mugger left firecrackers."

"What?"

Raina held up the little red package. Her family set off several strands of these in front of the house every Chinese New Year to ward off evil spirits.

"Do you think the mugger purposely attacked you for the journal? Maybe we should sic Weeping May on him."

Raina settled back on her heels, feeling the energy drain out of her. No freaking way. But it was the only thing that made any sense. If not for the return of the purse, she would have written off the incident at the BART station as nothing more than big city crime.

"Is the mugger trying to ward off the evil inside the journal? Or are the firecrackers to ward off my evil thoughts? Or is it a calling card?" Not that Raina had any kind of power to explode someone's head just from her thoughts alone.

"There aren't any recent crimes on the news involving

firecrackers. No, I think the firecrackers are directly linked to our little family drama."

Raina considered her options. She could either hide in the house, pretending the return of the purse was a lucky coincidence, or chase the journal's secrets until she fell into a rabbit hole. Neither was much of a choice, but there was her grandma to consider.

The three-million-dollar inheritance was an albatross. Her sister and cousins believed Raina had influenced their dying grandfather to change his will. It broke the fragile relationships she had with her family and forced her to leave the city. No, her grandma wasn't the only victim who needed closure.

"What are you planning to do?" Po Po's voice held a hint of anxiety. "That mulish look always means trouble."

"We need closure," Raina whispered.

The lucky cat clock ticked, filling the silence between them.

Po Po gave Raina a deer in headlights look. "I need to unpack." She hurried out of the kitchen.

Raina followed her grandma, reaching for the suitcase handle. They were silent on the way up, each lost in their own thoughts. Her grandma didn't need to unpack. It was an excuse to delay their much-needed talk.

Last Christmas, Po Po finally admitted to being mad at Raina for hiding Ah Gong's infidelity. As if by not saying anything, Raina had approved of her grandfather's behavior even though she hadn't known about it until the week before he'd passed on.

She still believed Po Po wouldn't have been able to handle the truth at the time of her husband's death. By keeping the secret, she had given her grandma time to grieve without questioning everything in her marriage, like she did now.

Raina set the suitcase on her grandma's bed. The bedroom was much as she'd remembered from her childhood. An orchid-print comforter with matching orchid curtains. A mother-of-pearl inlaid rosewood dressing table with matching stool and mirror that her grandma had brought with her from Hong Kong when she immigrated to the U.S. as a new bride. And yet, the room was different. There were still framed photos of the family, but gone were the photos of her grandparents together as a couple.

She swallowed the lump in her throat. As much as she wanted to believe otherwise, her grandfather's secret family in China would ravage the Wong family when everyone found out.

"I...I'm afraid," Po Po whispered. Her grandma clutched a pair of pajamas, twisting the gray silk into a laundress's nightmare. "How can you share a bed for fifty years and never suspect he was in love with another woman?" Her tone was as flat as her eyes.

Raina didn't know what to say. There were only two possible responses to the question—either her grandma was a fool or things were not what they appeared. She had no idea which was worse, but she was a fool for waving the journal like a banner at the party.

"I need to sort out this family secret. I could never move forward with this shadow hanging over me." Po Po glanced at Raina. "I need you to help me. I can't do this by myself."

Raina blinked at the tears burning in the back of her eyes. She hugged her grandma, rubbing the thin shoulders. Po Po sighed and returned the hug. As if a magician had just waved a wand over the pair, Raina's world was normal again.

A FEW MINUTES LATER, Po Po dropped the pretense of unpacking and they headed into the kitchen to have a brainstorming session with Ben and Jerry. There was no problem Chunky Monkey couldn't solve. One carton two spoons, just as Raina remembered from her childhood. All this traipsing up and down the stairs made her hungry.

"Where are you supposed to send the money?" Po Po asked.

"To a bank in China." Raina licked the spoon to delay explaining why she didn't look into the logistics of transferring the three million dollars to the other family. "I have no idea whether they needed the money to live on. And I'm ashamed to say I haven't sent them a cent." She gave her grandma a rueful smile. "I was hoping the problem would...disappear."

"I thought we were happy all these years," Po Po mumbled into the carton. "I need to stop feeling like a victim."

Raina dug her spoon into the ice cream in frustration. "I guess we need to pump Uncle Martin for information." The idea had just as much appeal as putting on someone's sweat-soaked shirt, but it had to be done in this case. If Uncle Martin put the move on Po Po in front of her, Raina would turn on the fire hydrant. Yuck!

Po Po blinked, a slow smile spreading across her face.

"Of course! Let's go." She dropped her spoon into the sink and hurled the ice cream carton back into the freezer.

Raina clutched her spoon in front of her, suddenly afraid. Should they have a game plan in case they dug up more than they could handle? "Do you like him?" she asked, stalling.

"We wouldn't be friends if I didn't."

If Raina showed up with Po Po, did it mean she struck a deal with Uncle Martin? Should she warn Po Po since her grandma was oblivious to his continued interest?

The front door rattled, accompanied by voices and laughter. The Victorian didn't have the open floor plan in modern homes, so it took another minute before Mom and Hudson appeared in the kitchen.

She looked flustered and taken aback to see both Raina and Po Po waiting expectantly at their entrance. "Oh." She laughed, a silly little giggle that tested Raina's willpower to keep her eyes from rolling.

Raina knew she was acting like a brat around her mom, but it was hard to respect a parent who acted like a teenager. She didn't begrudge her mom for having a boyfriend. It had been over ten years since her dad's death and she didn't deserve to be alone for the rest of her life. No, it wasn't the boyfriend that Raina objected to —it was the lack of interest in anyone else.

Hudson smiled at the audience. "Hi, Wong Po Po." He nodded at Raina, who returned the greeting in kind.

"Po Po, I hope you don't mind, but I invited Hudson to the New Year's Eve dinner," Mom said.

Raina gave them a tight-lipped smile. It was traditional for family members to have a big dinner on Chinese New Year's Eve to signify they would spend the upcoming year together as a happy family. For Mom to want to spend the evening with Hudson meant they were beyond the casual dating phase. Were they planning to announce an engagement?

"Not a problem," Po Po said with a smile like she just got electrocuted. "Is Martin home this evening?"

"I'm not sure," Hudson said. "Why?"

Uncle Martin didn't own a cell phone. They would have to track him down the old fashioned way—by ringing the house phone until someone picked up.

Po Po shook her head. "I want to find someone to walk down memory lane. There aren't that many people who knew Ah Gong as a young man."

"Why are you thinking about Dad, Po Po?" Mom asked.

"I wondered what he did in China when he still wanted to save the world."

The front door opened. Once again, laughing voices and thumps as heavy bags hit the floor. Win appeared with his girlfriend in tow. Mom's lips tightened into a thin line at the midriff-baring T-shirt on the girlfriend. Win and his girlfriend mumbled greetings, grabbed food from the refrigerator and disappeared into the living room.

Raina whispered to Po Po, "Let's get out of here before someone asks about dinner."

4

———

BLEACH MY EARS

R aina glanced up at the three-story townhouse. The interior lights were off. "I thought you said he's home." The front light lit the small porch, spotlighting the two of them like they were on a stage.

Po Po pressed the doorbell again, leaning into the old-fashioned buzzer. "That's what he said on the phone." She grabbed the bug screen on the window next to the porch, tugging it off the frame.

"What are you doing?" Raina glanced up and down the street. "What if the neighbors think we're breaking in?"

Po Po handed the screen to Raina. "I'm his hot young trophy girlfriend. They'll just think ditsy me forgot my keys."

Raina ignored the comment about Po Po's age. Her grandma's voodoo math would have made her a decade younger than Uncle Martin even though she got the senior discount years earlier. "I don't think they could tell

37

his girlfriend from a burglar when all they see is your behind hanging out."

"You got a point there." Po Po cupped her hands. "Your behind is skinnier, so up you go."

Raina held the screen in front of her. "I'm not going up there." At her grandma's disappointed look, she added, "Let's see if there's a side window."

By the time she replaced the bug screen, her grandma had already disappeared around the side of the house. She groaned, but trotted after her grandma, who appeared to need this ninja act to get over the emotional scene earlier.

Uncle Martin's townhouse was a corner unit, which came with a luxurious four-feet-by-six-feet side yard, which commanded an additional twenty thousand dollars, or so they had been told. There was just enough room so he didn't have to store his trashcans in the garage like the rest of his neighbors. The hinges squealed when Raina pushed open the gate.

Po Po teetered on the lid of the trashcan as she peered into a darkened window. Raina rushed forward, hoping to steady her grandma. Her legs shot out from underneath her, just as rancid tomatoes hit her nostrils. Her arms flung out, banging against the trashcan, and her back slammed into the paved patio at the same time her grandma toppled onto Raina's stomach. The trashcan clattered against the side of the house.

As Po Po slid off, Raina curled into a fetal position. Twice in less than forty-eight hours. She would spend the Year of the Monkey flat on her back without a man anywhere in sight.

"Rainy?" Po Po patted her face. "Are you okay?"

Raina brushed off the exploring hands and rolled into a sitting position. Damp liquid seeped through her pants. Rotten tomatoes. Yuck.

The light came on in the side window. "So Uncle Martin is home. It would have been much easier if we had kept banging on the door," Raina said.

Uncle Martin was talking to his neighbor by the time Raina and Po Po turned to the front. He introduced the pair to Mrs. Keane, a woman in her late sixties with a tight perm and even tighter face. The yipping Boston terrier in her arms looked as if he needed a fire hydrant.

Mrs. Keane's gaze traveled the length of Raina and dismissed her with a sniff. Her eyes narrowed as she studied Po Po. "Oh, Marty, your friends gave Gigi a heart attack. A single woman can't be too careful with the riffraff in the city." She glanced down demurely. "Quiet, Gigi. These are friends of Marty."

Uncle Martin didn't notice the smoldering look Mrs. Keane gave him from beneath her lashes. He smiled at Po Po, his eyes twinkling as if he got a treat. "We'll get out of your way. Sorry about Gigi."

A few minutes later, Raina munched on an almond cookie in a living room straight out of the '60s—dark wood paneling covered an entire wall, shag carpeting that probably held several decades worth of dead skin cells, and bright geometric prints which competed with framed photos of his niece and nephew. She glanced at her hands just to give her eyes a break.

Her tailbone ached. The fall had finished off what the BART station incident had started. Was this the beginning of a bad luck streak?

Po Po and Uncle Martin were chatting away like the

old friends they were. He kept throwing sideways glances at Raina as if she could read his mind. He wiggled his eyebrows, causing the shaggy hair to twitch like a dead centipede.

"Are your eyes okay?" Po Po finally asked.

Uncle Martin reddened. "No. Everything is fine." He held out the teapot to Raina. "Why don't you go get us more hot water?"

Po Po reached for the teapot. "I can do it. Rainy shouldn't be moving yet." She headed toward the kitchen, winking at Raina when she walked past Uncle Martin. "Distract him," she mouthed. She pointed at herself and then jerked a thumb toward the hallway behind her.

Raina's heart sank. Her grandma was planning to snoop.

Uncle Martin waited a heartbeat and whipped his head around to make sure Po Po cleared the room. He patted Raina's hand. "Good job, dear. Now I need you to leave us alone for a few minutes so I can ask her out."

"Do you want me to hide in the bathroom or something?" Raina asked.

Uncle Martin beamed as if she was a bright pupil. "Perfect. Make it a diarrhea attack so you can stay in there at least fifteen minutes."

She cleared her throat. Here was the opening she needed. "So what happened with Ah Gong in China? What can you tell me about his mistress?"

"What mistress?"

"Didn't Ah Gong get himself a mistress in nineteen sixty two?" Raina's gaze darted to the hallway that led to the rest of the house. "I'm leaving with Po Po if you don't uphold your end of the bargain."

Uncle Martin gave her a look, half exasperated and half amused. "He was part of the Beijing contingent who visited my village to check on the yield after implementing their version of Western agricultural ideas. What did the paper pushers from the city know about farming? The elders made us transplant the rice seedlings from three nearby villages into this one field for the visit. The rest of the party left happy at the prospect of an excellent harvest, but he wasn't convinced." He closed his eyes as a flash of terror crossed his face. "He stayed behind and learned to regret the decision."

Raina's mouth grew dry at his reaction. The almond cookie stuck to the back of her throat. Did she want to open this can of worms? As she sipped the hot tea, she pondered the question. Not only was the can already opened, the squirming invertebrates were dumped into her underwear drawer.

Uncle Martin opened his eyes. "Since that winter, I can't sleep. I need my sleeping draught every night, no matter how exhausted I am." He smiled. "But Bonnie helped your Ah Gong sleep all these years. I'm hoping she can work her magic on me."

And just like that, the spell was broken. Raina wanted to cover her ears and say la-la-la. Yuck!

"How's the family business?" she asked, not with any real interest. As a well-known Feng Shui Master, Uncle Martin was much in demand in the Chinese community.

"Hudson is struggling with the nuances," Uncle Martin said diplomatically. "I'm sure it'll work out fine. And if not, I will be dead so I won't see the business close its doors."

Raina wasn't sure if his attitude toward mortality

aligned with her grandma's zest for life. She had grown up with Uncle Martin as part of the family, but she had paid no more attention to him than she did the furniture. He was just there. "Do you like the thing between my mother and your nephew?"

"I wouldn't call their relationship a 'thing.' Does it bother you?"

Raina didn't want to talk about her relationship with her mother. "Why don't you look for a new hobby? Trust me, it's much easier than dating."

"Bonnie is my new hobby." Uncle Martin chuckled. His eyes disappeared into the loose skin around them.

Yuck.

Po Po returned to the living room without the teapot. Her face was pale, and she moved stiffly. "I need to go. Stomach problems." Uncle Martin reached for her, and she jerked away from him.

Raina frowned, shifting her gaze between the two of them. What did her grandma find in the back of the house? A dead body?

Before she could react, someone used the front door knocker. The sound echoed in the silent living room. As Uncle Martin got up to answer the door, Po Po gathered her purse and jacket. She averted her gaze, so Raina couldn't even whisper a reassuring comment to her grandma.

Hudson and Mom stepped into the room with take-out bags from a restaurant. There was a traffic jam at the doorway as Po Po and Raina tried to leave while the other three shuffled to make room for them.

"Leaving already? We got enough food for the five of us," Mom said.

"Stay for a bit," Hudson said. "We've got good egg rolls."

Raina sneaked a sideways glance at Po Po. Her grandma's face had a pinched expression that worried her. "Sorry, I have to go. Stomach problems. I don't want to clog up Uncle Martin's toilet." And with that, they hustled outside.

RAINA BOLTED off her bed and landed in a crouch. As she swiveled her head, her heart hammered in her chest. The rustling noise drifted in again from the other side of the guest bedroom door. A quick glance at the radio clock revealed it was six in the morning. She grabbed her robe and padded silently into the hall. The faint laughter drifting upstairs from the dining room suggested mischief-makers rather than cat burglars.

If Mom caught Win trying to sneak his girlfriend into his room again, it would be World War III. While Raina was young enough to remember the rush of hormones, it didn't make things any less awkward when she'd walked in on half-dressed teenagers on the sofa on her first day back to her childhood home.

She squinted at the two dark shapes at the far side of the dining table. The weak morning light filtered through the lace curtains from behind them, leaving their faces in shadows. The remnants on the table suggested that someone had the munchies— take-out containers, a bottle of wine, and several sauce packets.

The laughter stopped when they noticed Raina standing at the entryway. While she couldn't make out who was at the table, they could see her perfectly. Did they expect Raina to disappear if they stayed quiet? The silence stretched until a car backfired outside, startling the woman into knocking over the wine glass. The man grabbed a napkin and blotted at the woman's lap.

"It's okay." Mom grabbed her boyfriend's hands and her voice sounded embarrassed. And why shouldn't she be? She would throw a fit if her son were in a similar situation. The apple didn't fall far from the tree.

"Good morning, Mom." Raina turned to leave but paused for a heartbeat. "Or is it good night?" So she wasn't on the fast track to sainthood. It certainly was worth it. If only she could have seen her mother's face. She couldn't believe Mom and Hudson were still up. Geez, even teenagers behaved better.

On the way back to the guest room, Raina stopped outside of Po Po's bedroom. She pressed an ear to the door and heard faint snoring. Good. Her grandma was getting some much-needed rest.

During the ride home from Uncle Martin's townhouse last evening, Po Po had stared out the darkened passenger window. Raina hadn't pressed her grandma at the time, but she intended to do so over breakfast. She yawned and stumbled back into bed. By the time Raina woke up at a proper hour, Po Po was long gone.

Raina tried calling her grandma's cell phone number, but it went straight to voicemail. She sipped her tasteless coffee, staring at the waffles on her plate.

Where would her grandma go at eight in the morning? Her two favorite senior centers didn't open before ten. Whatever had upset her grandma originated from

Uncle Martin's house. Maybe a look-see in his house could give Raina a clue.

She grabbed the cordless phone again, dialing Uncle Martin's number. The phone rang and rang. Another dead end.

Or would this be a good time to snoop with Uncle Martin out of the way? She could call again once she got to Richmond District. After all, Uncle Martin was an elderly man living alone. She got concerned when she couldn't reach him, so she had to climb in through his side window to check up on him.

Raina parked five blocks away, just to ensure no one in the neighborhood could identify her car, especially that Mrs. Keane with the yipping Gigi.

Besides, Raina needed the exercise. She had fallen out of her regular running routine. After seeing the changes in Hudson Rice, she didn't want to end up like one of those stick figure cartoons with a circle for her stomach.

As she turned the corner, the noise volume increased. Several emergency vehicles clogged the narrow street. A handful of neighbors clustered together, talking and pointing at the official-looking people coming and going from Uncle Martin's townhouse.

Mrs. Keane spoke to a man with a face sharp as a hatchet on the landing outside her front door. As if on a stage, the pair stood one story above the crowd, but they ignored their audience. From the way he was taking notes, Raina assumed he must be a plainclothes cop.

She had to force herself to take slow measured steps toward the onlookers. A couple of them glanced at her, but they continued to whisper to each other. She kept her expression blank while she listened to the chatter.

"... died in his sleep..."

"... older than the hills."

"... no kids..."

"...his niece...nice girl."

"...haven't seen her in a year...just the brother."

A lump formed in Raina's throat. Uncle Martin was dead? She shook her head. No way. She spoke with him last night. She blinked, and the scene before her became whitewashed like the sun had leached out all the colors.

Mrs. Keane studied the crowd. Her arm rose, and she pointed at Raina. The hatchet-faced cop turned his head to follow her finger.

5

———

TWENTY-ONE HOURS

As gooseflesh peppered her arms, Raina shivered at the chill she saw behind the hatchet-faced cop's steel gray eyes. The sun offered no warmth or shadow to hide beneath. As if on cue, the crowd parted until she was the only actor standing under a spotlight.

Raina swallowed the fear that rose in her throat. She had done nothing wrong. She wasn't someone the police would be interested in.

The hatchet-faced cop slipped his notebook back into his jacket and headed straight toward Raina. By the time he stood in front of her, the crowd disappeared, as if they could be found guilty by association. Mrs. Keane trailed after him, holding Gigi, who yipped within sneezing distance from Raina.

Mrs. Keane looked her full sixty years. Her tears left streaks on her foundation. Her swollen red eyes made the wrinkles around her mouth appear deep enough to hide gravel.

Raina focused on the glint she saw behind the neighbor's red eyes. This was no time for her to give in to tears of her own. She had seen those calculating eyes directed at her grandma when the neighbor thought she had a romantic rival.

The hatchet-faced cop studied Raina like he had already labeled her. Chinese girl. Size of a pygmy goat. No threat. He probably thought her naturally curly hair was a bad perm like everyone else did.

Like he won the lottery in the looks department. The cop was a pipsqueak of a man, maybe five-four if she was generous. His clothes were tight as if he wanted to show off what little muscle he had.

"What's going on? Why are these people at Uncle Martin's house..." Raina swallowed, unable to finish.

Mrs. Keane let out a loud keening wail. Gigi leaped out of her arms and pressed her quivering body against Raina's legs. Even she seemed cowed by the howl coming from her owner. An officer put an arm around Mrs. Keane and led her away. You would think she was the widow by the way she carried on.

The hatchet-faced cop guided Raina to the opened door of a marked vehicle and sat her on the seat. "Deep breaths. In and out." His voice was routine and cold like he was on autopilot.

Raina hunched over her knees, gulping air. In. Out. She swallowed and focused on the oil stain on the road. "I'm fine," she repeated through numb lips.

A warm blanket enveloped her. She glanced up to find the hatchet-faced cop still studying her. No concern. No warmth. An automaton doing his duty. She shuddered, glad she hadn't become jaded by death like the man who stood before her.

"Is Uncle Martin dead?" she asked.

"I'm sorry, ma'am. He was found dead this morning," the hatchet-faced cop said. "Is he a relative?"

Raina blinked at the tears in her eyes. "A family friend. I've known him my entire life. I need to call my grandma."

"Would she be Bonnie Wong?"

The hair on the back of Raina's neck stiffened, warning her of impending danger. "And you are?"

He flashed a badge so fast, a person couldn't tell the difference between it and a movie prop. "I'm Detective Smith. Mrs. Keane was telling me you visited your uncle last night."

Raina didn't like the way he said "uncle" as if to imply there was more to the story than what she'd already told. "As did other people. What's your point?"

"There's no need to get defensive. I'm just making conversation."

"I'm sorry, but now is not the time for a chat. A man I've known my entire life is..." Her voice cracked, and she snapped her mouth shut to prevent further display of her turbulent emotions. With Uncle Martin dead and the journal gone, how was she to find out how her grandfather ended up with a secret family? She immediately felt shame for thinking about herself.

"As much as it pains me, I need to ask you some questions," Smith said. "What is your name and contact information?"

She stared at him with a mulish expression. What a jerk.

"Either you cooperate or I can take you to the station for questioning."

Raina knew she had little choice, but he didn't have to sound so smug. "Can I see your badge again?" She held out her hand so he couldn't do the quick flash.

He seemed puzzled by her request but handed over his badge.

She whipped out her cell phone and took a photo.

"Hey! What are you doing?" Smith demanded.

Raina handed back his badge. "I have a bad memory. I want to make sure I got your badge number right when I write my letter to the police commissioner about the way you treat grieving family members. Now what are your questions?"

"Lady, I'm just doing my job." He jammed the badge back into his jacket pocket. "What is your name and contact info?"

Raina's cell phone dinged at an incoming text message. She ignored it.

"I can wait if you need to check your phone," Smith said.

Raina didn't trust he wouldn't try to look over her shoulder while she replied. "It can wait." She answered his routine questions for the next thirty minutes.

Smith snapped his notebook shut. "See, it wasn't so bad, was it? I may have some follow-up questions later on. Thank you for your time, Miss Sun."

Raina got up, leaving the blanket on the seat of the police vehicle. The crowd had thinned. One person with a white hoodie watched the officers finish up. When he turned, she saw the flash of a scar on his mouth—the mugger from the BART station.

"Hey! You in the white hoodie!" Raina called out, rushing toward him.

He glanced at her and took off.

Smith called out, "Don't let the white hoodie get away." His longer legs carried him past her.

By the time she got to the corner, Scar Face was long gone. Smith straightened and shoved his hand into his jacket pocket. He glared at the cars and pedestrians clogging the intersection.

"Who was that guy?" Smith asked.

Raina bent over, resting her hands on her knees. She took a deep breath. Boy, she was out of shape. "I thought he was the guy who mugged me last night."

"What? You made me chase a guy for three blocks over a petty crime?"

"I didn't ask you to. I can't help it if you gave chase like a dumb bonehead." She grimaced mentally as the words left her mouth. Geez, she shouldn't have said that.

"I have a feeling we're going to see a lot of each other."

Her cell phone dinged again.

He glanced at her purse.

Her phone rang.

Without breaking eye contact, Raina grabbed her phone. "Hello?"

"Raina—"

"Mom, I can't talk right now." She hung up. Another ding.

"Must be important if your mom is trying so hard to contact you. Need a police escort?" Smith asked.

"Am I free to go?"

"One more question—how can I get in touch with Bonnie Wong?"

"I don't know."

"Tell her I'll be by the house tomorrow."

"I—"

"You're too young to have the money to live on Pacific Heights. Must be a family home."

Raina waited until he was heading back to Uncle Martin's house before pulling out her cell phone to check her messages.

The next-door neighbor posted Uncle Martin's death on Facebook. Hudson is beside himself. Help!

The drive to the Sunset District took ten minutes, but she took another five to find parking. She ended up eight blocks further than her last spot. She might have been better off just walking to Hudson's apartment.

The change in weather was significant in those blocks. The thick fog hunkered in this low area like a squatter. Raina jammed her hands into her pockets and marched without seeing more than ten feet ahead of her. She passed cafes and shops with flashing "Open" signs and condensation on their windows. People were out and about, but she saw only one or two at a time before they disappeared from sight.

She felt numb but wasn't sure if it was from the chill or the news of Uncle Martin's death. At the thought of finding her mom prostrate with grief at Hudson's, Raina's feet slowed even though her destination was the next building over. Her stomach rumbled, reminding her she'd missed lunch.

Should she keep walking to the cafe at the end of the block and duck in for a quick bite? Would this make her a horrible daughter?

A woman bumped into Raina from behind.

As Raina straightened, she called out, "Hey, watch where you're going!"

The woman didn't even glance at her. She jammed a finger on the buzzer to Hudson's apartment building. When the outer door clicked open, she disappeared inside. Raina did the same and stormed up the stairs to the second floor. She heard the screaming match before she saw the participants.

"You will not get away with this," a woman said. "I'm going to the police—"

"Stop! We do not understand what happened. For all we know, Uncle Martin could have died in his sleep," Hudson said, his voice sounding clogged and congested like he had been crying. "Brandi, just go home. I'll call you later and we can talk then."

Raina rounded the corner on the second floor. The woman who had bumped into her stood with clenched fists outside an apartment. Mom, with her hands on her hips, shielded Hudson with her body.

"It's all over Facebook and Instagram. The next-door neighbor is a minor celebrity because she found the body with you this morning," Brandi said. "I can't believe you were stupid enough to involve the old busybody."

Raina studied the rude woman. The Asian genes from their mom's side bypassed Brandi Rice, Hudson's older sister. She was a petite brunette with ice blue eyes. The bruise on her cheek was ripe like a plum with the edges turning yellow.

"She has the spare key. How else could I have gotten into his place?" he said.

A neighbor popped his head out of his unit, but when Brandi gave him the finger, he jerked back inside.

"If this is how you want to play this, Hudson, we can both go down in flames. My lawyer will tie everything in probate, so we will both end up with nothing." Brandi gave a brittle laugh that could have been a cackle, except she cut it short and spun on her heels.

Raina huddled against the wall so she wouldn't get bumped again.

As Brandi rushed past, she blinked rapidly, but this didn't stop the tears from spilling down her cheeks.

MOM PUT an arm around Hudson's hunched shoulders. She turned her head and mouthed "wait here." The two of them disappeared inside the apartment.

Raina jammed her hands into her pockets and paced in the hall. Death brought out the worst in some people, but to have the Rice siblings squabbling already was not good news.

Mom came out, closing the door quietly behind her. "I need your help. Brandi will do everything in her power to make trouble for Hudson. I think she'll implicate him somehow."

Raina studied the fifty-year-old woman in front of her. The hair started to gray in the last year, streaking her black hair, but she was still trim and youthful enough to pass for forty. Her oval face seemed puffy as if she'd been crying. "I don't understand. Anybody can make a wild accusation. It doesn't mean the police would make trouble for your boyfriend."

Mom pleaded with her eyes. "I need him to be more than my boyfriend. I don't think he will propose until everything is settled with Uncle Martin's death."

Raina took a deep breath to keep her voice from sounding dismissive. "I still don't understand what you want me to do."

"What you do best—poke your nose into Uncle Martin's death. I want this settled ASAP so Hudson can finish his mourning and propose to me. My future happiness is at stake here."

"Don't you think you're jumping the gun? Why don't we wait until the coroner comes back with the cause of death?"

"I'm disappointed that you are refusing to help me. I guess twenty-one hours of labor without medication doesn't count for much these days."

Raina shuffled her feet and tried not to snap at her mom. Did she have to pull the labor card?

As if sensing her imminent victory, Mom gestured for Raina to follow her inside Hudson's apartment. "Come and talk to Hudson. He'll convince you there's something fishy about Uncle Martin's death, but I don't want him to know you're investigating. That would be too presumptuous."

6

IN THE DOGHOUSE

Raina took longer than necessary to close the door. The apartment was nothing more than a one-bedroom studio, much smaller than her place in Gold Springs, but cost four times as much in rent. A curtain sectioned off the bed from the rest of the space, which was comprised of a loveseat and a coffee table that also doubled as a dining room table. Since there was no other seat, Raina sat on the rug next to the coffee table.

On the loveseat, Hudson hung his head over his knees. His gaze focused inward. Mom rubbed his back in silence.

After a couple of minutes, Raina cleared her throat. "I'm sorry about Uncle Martin. What happened?"

Hudson's hands trembled, and he tucked them under his armpits. "Uncle Martin and I have dim sum every Tuesday morning, but when he didn't show up, I stopped by his home. Mrs. Keane let me in..." He took a shuddering breath. "He was fine when we left last night. I don't understand what happened. I should have stayed with him."

Mom patted Hudson's knee. "It's not your fault. If there were anyone to blame, it would be me. If I ate more dinner, then you wouldn't have had to make a snack run."

The image of Mom and Hudson necking in the dining room in the wee hours of the morning floated across Raina's mind and she quickly suppressed it. "What did you see when you walked into the townhouse?"

"Mrs. Keane and I went inside, calling out for Uncle Martin. At first, I thought he was asleep because he was still sitting on the sofa. It wasn't until she screamed that I realized something was wrong. He was too still." Hudson pressed his trembling lips together. Several seconds passed before he could continue. And when he did, his voice came out in a raspy whisper. "Except his bloodshot eyes were wide open."

Mom gasped and her hand flew to her mouth. "Poor baby."

"Then what happened?" Raina asked, ignoring her mom. Did he have a heart attack?

"I don't remember. Someone must have called the police because the next thing I knew there were a bunch of people at the house. Mrs. Keane later told me that I picked up the crane pillow and set it back on the sofa." Hudson blinked, his eyes clouded with confusion. "Brandi will tell the police I killed him. I just know it. It's not my fault Uncle Martin reduced her inheritance to five thousand dollars."

"Oh, poor baby," Mom said, rubbing his back.

Raina rubbed her temples. One more "poor baby," and she would scream. "Mom, why don't you make

Hudson a cup of tea?" She tilted her head toward the kitchenette.

Mom brightened at the idea and hurried off.

Raina turned back to Hudson. "Is there something unnatural about Uncle Martin's death?"

Hudson hugged himself tighter. "I heard Detective Smith whisper to an officer that Uncle Martin probably died from asphyxiation."

Raina glanced at her mom to give him a moment to collect himself. Though Smith wasn't a coroner, she didn't doubt his experience to judge whether a crime had occurred. "Did Uncle Martin take his usual sleeping draught? He mentioned last night he'd had trouble sleeping for years. Is there any possibility he could have overdosed on it?"

"He had been taking the herbal remedy for decades. There was no way he could have OD'd on it."

"Where did he get the ingredients? I wonder if he got a bad batch."

Hudson shook his head. "The Chinese apothecary has been in business for fifty years. Their prices are higher than everyone else, but they have a reputation for quality ingredients. I can't think of the name, but it's off the side street from the Golden Gate Bakery."

Mom returned with two cups of tea and handed one to Hudson. He thanked her and rested it on his knees. She blew on hers and sipped it.

Raina ignored the fact she didn't get a cup. "What did your sister mean about going to the police?"

"She's just upset at Uncle Martin's death. They used to be close until the loser boyfriend came into the picture. She wouldn't leave him, so Uncle Martin cut her off the will, hoping the boyfriend would go away when he realized Brandi had no money coming."

"It didn't work?"

Hudson shook his head.

"Is it possible someone murdered Uncle Martin?" Raina asked.

Hudson's eyes jerked, and his cup slipped from his hands. Mom jumped up, running into the kitchen for paper towels. It took a couple of minutes to clean up the mess.

He raked a hand through his hair. "Sorry about that. Your question surprised me."

"Asphyxiation rarely happens by itself."

"Why would anyone kill Uncle Martin?"

"What about angry clients? Is there anyone that might be unhappy with his work? When you are working with ancestors, some people could get mighty touchy."

Hudson frowned, staring off into space for several moments. "There's the Dai Lo from the Nine Dragons, but I don't think you should talk to him."

The name sounded oddly familiar, but Raina wasn't sure where she'd heard it before. "Why not?"

"Because he's a Dai Lo," Mom said, emphasizing the title in Cantonese.

A light bulb went off in Raina's head. The literal translation meant big brother in slang, but Dai Lo was also the title used by underlings to address a triad boss.

No wonder the Nine Dragons sounded so familiar. It was on the news a few days ago that a member who'd hounded Chinese businesses for protection money in the East Bay was released from prison. "I second that motion.

Can you think of anyone who might have a grudge against Uncle Martin?"

Hudson frowned, beginning to shake his head, but his eyes widened at a sudden thought. "His business rival —Joley Mok. She opened a feng shui shop in Chinatown two years ago. Uncle Martin asserted she was too young to be a master. They even argued publicly last year when the Chinatown Business Association wanted to re-align the feng shui in their lobby. Uncle Martin called her a hack and she called him an old fool. Someone else ended up with the contract. Several clients canceled on her afterward."

Mom set her teacup on the coffee table. "What do you think, Raina?"

"You're better off hiring a pro," Raina said.

Mom shook her head. "We have to keep this in the family."

Raina chewed on her lower lip. She was absolutely right. The feng shui business relied on word of mouth and a belief in superstition. Potential clients getting wind of the "bad luck" surrounding Uncle Martin's death meant the family business would be toast.

Hudson's head swiveled between Raina and her mom. "What am I missing?"

Mom patted his hand. "Don't worry about it, dear. You need to focus on putting together the memorial service. Just let me take care of us."

Raina didn't want to be responsible for the survival of someone's livelihood. What if there was no more sleuthing mojo left in her reserve? But this could be a chance to mend fences with her mom even though the coldness between them wasn't Raina's fault to begin with. "Fine, but I'm not promising anything."

IN THE LOBBY of Hudson's building, Raina dialed her grandma's cell number, glancing out the main door. Through the glass, she saw Smith approaching the building.

It didn't take a rocket scientist to know Smith wanted to chat with Hudson. It wouldn't take long for the detective to cross her path again. Better to delay the happy event as long as possible.

She hung up and strolled down the short hallway which led to the four units downstairs. The lobby door opened and a draft swirled around the small area, lifting a few strands of her curly hair. At the farthest apartment, Raina dug into her purse, pretending to look for her keys.

When she could no longer hear the footsteps on the stairs, she risked peeking out from underneath her hair. The lobby was empty. She sprinted for the main door, grabbed the handle, and flew onto the street.

Raina trotted several blocks, just to make sure she was out of sight and called her grandmother again. As the phone rang, she studied the strips of cha siu hanging over the butcher block on the other side of the window at a restaurant. The Chinese style barbecue pork glistened in the late evening light.

Her stomach rumbled, and she felt a wave of light-headedness. The last time she ate was breakfast. She hung up and stepped inside to order a cha siu rice plate.

While she ate, Raina called her grandmother's two

favorite senior centers, but no one had seen Po Po. Finally, in a moment of desperation, she checked her grandma's Facebook feed. Po Po had updated it less than two hours ago.

IN THE DOG HOUSE. NEED FOOD.

Raina paused mid-sip—one hand held the glass of water suspended in front of her while the other held her phone. Did Po Po mean with the police or...was she in their backyard? The ice water leaked around the side of her mouth and soaked the top of her shirt. She set the glass down, still reading the updates on her phone and blotting at her shirt absentmindedly.

Po Po must have read Mrs. Keane's postings on the Internet and went into hiding mode. Raina wasn't sure why, but a dog house was exactly the place her grandma would choose. This streak for the theatrics made everyone exasperated with the matriarch of the family.

Raina ordered another cha siu rice plate to go. She got back to the house in record time and went into the house and headed straight out the back door.

The Wong family didn't own a dog, but they owned a dog house which served as their hiding place for their spare key. Anyone who disregarded their "Beware of Dog" sign and opened their side yard gate could see the doghouse and hear a pre-recorded Rottweiler barking.

"Cha siu faahn," Raina whispered in a singsong voice. "Cha siu faahn. Who wants dinner?"

The literal translation of Chinese phrases always puzzled the next-door neighbors, a young Caucasian family trying to learn the native language of their adopted daughter. If they had heard her, they would assume she had poured the cha siu sauce over her rice.

"Pssst," a voice hissed from inside the doghouse.

Raina's shoulders sagged in relief. "I'm heading back into the kitchen to put the food on a plate. You can follow me if you want or you can stay out here all night." She strolled back into the kitchen, knowing full well her grandma would follow. She scraped the Chinese food out of the take-out boxes and put it on a plate.

Po Po stomped into the kitchen and locked the back door. "Thanks for picking up dinner."

"Why were you hiding in the doghouse?"

Po Po gave her a pitying look. "Oh, honey, no wonder you were an engineer. You have no pizzazz. Now I can tell my friends I was out in the cold and dark, hiding from the police, who would beat the truth out of me if I was caught."

Raina handed the plate to her grandma. "Eat. We'll talk later. I'm taking a shower."

An hour later Raina was sprawled on her grandma's bed while Po Po changed into her pajamas. Neither Mom nor Win was home yet. Raina wondered if she should be worried her teenage brother had unlimited freedom to come and go as he pleased. She had always known her mom would never win any parental award, but how difficult was it to set a curfew on a school night?

A flash of annoyance shot through her. Why was it she always ended up doing her mom's job? When Dad died, Raina had lost more than just a parent—she'd lost her childhood as well. With both her mom and older sister falling apart and her half-sister taking off on her own, Raina became the glue that held the family together.

"Rainy? Are you okay?" Po Po asked.

Raina shook the thoughts from her head. Water under the bridge now.

"No?" Po Po asked.

"It's Mom, but I don't want to talk about it right now."

"I'm sorry I didn't do a good job as a parent."

"Will you stop being the martyr? You know my relationship with my mother has nothing to do with you."

"If I didn't—"

"No, we are not having this discussion tonight. We can't change her, so there's no point in going around in circles and wasting our mental energy on something beyond our control."

Raina took a deep breath to calm herself. She was getting worked up again. She seemed to fall into the same role of resentful daughter every time she stayed longer than a day in her childhood home. "Where did you go this morning? It had something to do with whatever you found at Uncle Martin's house last night."

Po Po clenched her jaw. The mulish expression settled in like an unwanted guest ready for a long visit. "I don't want to talk about this either."

Raina knew she wouldn't get anywhere with her questions. "Whatever happened to no more secrets? I guess it only applied to me."

"There's room for privacy in any relationship. If I want you to know, I will tell you when I'm ready."

Raina jerked her chin, which could be taken as a reluctant nod when one squinted. Whatever her grandma was hiding had to be ferreted out with finesse.

"What about hiding in a doghouse? Can we talk about this?"

"Not much to say. Mrs. Keane's tear-streaked face with a caption that said the love of her life, Martin Eng, just died in his sleep showed up on Instagram. That woman even posted a picture of Detective Smith, identifying him as the lead investigator. After I got over the initial shock, I knew the police would want to talk to me. I was walking up the street when I saw the detective with another officer at our front door. I backtracked and hopped over the fence from the neighbor's backyard."

Raina bit her lip to keep from laughing. Her great-grandma, Tai Po, had been an opera singer and actress prior to her elevation as third wife. Both Po Po and Mom didn't fall far from the tree according to her paternal grandmother. "I'm surprised you didn't break anything with such a maneuver. Couldn't you have waited until they left without taking such a drastic measure?"

Po Po tapped her smartphone and held it up. A fisheye view of the street came up. "There was a break-in after Ah Gong's death, and I installed video surveillance cameras around the house." She pinched the screen to zoom in on a vehicle. "Looks like an officer is still watching the house. It would have been a long wait if I didn't take my drastic measure."

7

———

CAT AND MOUSE

After updating her grandma about the arm twisting to get involved in the investigation, Raina called it a night. There wasn't much they could do other than rehash old news and circle treacherous topics.

Raina tossed and turned all night. Her dreams ranged from a glowing tome that drifted toward her like a holy book and dodging uniformed men. After discovering her childhood home had a sophisticated video surveillance system, she was more worried than reassured.

Having "beware of dog" signs and a doghouse when there was no dog were endearing and eccentric, but having actual surveillance bordered on paranoia. Or had Raina grown soft to the dangers of urban living?

She got up at six thirty to start breakfast for everyone. On her way downstairs, she peeked into her little brother's room to find him snoring like a chainsaw. At least he was in his own bed last night.

By the time the kitchen filled with the scents of

brewing coffee and fresh waffles, a flurry of activity upstairs—running water and banging cabinets—broke the stillness of the morning.

Win flew into the room with his backpack slung over one shoulder, and she held up a waffle and his travel cup full of hot chocolate. He stuffed the waffle in his mouth and left the house, banging the front door closed. Maybe things hadn't changed much around here after all.

As Raina refilled her mug, Po Po came into the room, thumping her cane and carrying a small backpack with a canteen attached to her waist. Her mane of silvery white hair was in a loose braid over the shoulder. Mountain granny ready to conquer the hills of San Francisco.

Raina eyed her grandma's accessories. It was no secret her grandma liked to play dress-up, but she forgot the point of a disguise—blending into a crowd.

"Where's your outfit, Rainy?" Po Po asked.

"Not planning to use one."

Po Po tapped on her cell phone. "Someone is still watching the house. We will not leave without a tail."

"I don't think a disguise would help. Why don't you call Mr. Clark and see if we could leave through his front door?" Mr. Clark's house faced the opposite street that ran parallel to theirs. "We can climb over the storage shed and drop into his yard."

Po Po brightened at the idea. "We could be like Rambo dropping in on enemy territory. I need to get my camo. Be back in a jiffy. I will also wake up Melody."

"Wait—"

Her grandma ran up the stairs and disappeared from view.

Raina tiptoed into the living room and peered out the window. A black Fiat was parked across from the house. The driver had the seat leaned all the way back as if he had been outside for a while. She bit her lip, studying him, but she couldn't make out the face in the dim interior of the car.

Something was off. The SFPD wouldn't have the manpower to post someone to watch a person of interest on a twenty-four-hour surveillance. She didn't want to alarm her family by bringing this up. The man pulled out a pair of binoculars, and Raina jerked back from the window.

She headed back to the kitchen to find Mom resting her chin on her hand, eyes closed. She swayed on the stool but seemed to catch her balance whenever she appeared close to tipping over.

Po Po hung up her cell phone. "I miss slamming a phone receiver. Tapping on a screen just doesn't have the same effect."

"I guess Mr. Clark hasn't forgiven you for killing his tree, huh?" Raina asked.

"He said we are forbidden"—Po Po made air quotes with her fingers around the last word—"to go into his yard even if he were dying of a heart attack." She made a show of preparing a cup of tea. "I didn't do it on purpose. It was not my fault the demons wanted to play in our backyard. I offered to pay for a replacement. Geez, the man is just too sensitive."

Mom cracked an eyelid to give Raina a significant look. After Ah Gong's death, Po Po went through a period where she thought she saw supernatural things. Salting the dirt around the forty-five-year-old tree planted by the now deceased Mrs. Clark appeared to be tame in comparison to some of the things she did.

"Clark leaves the house at nine o'clock on the dot every morning for the library so he can read the day's newspaper. Then he's at Subway for lunch." Po Po glanced at the lucky cat clock on the kitchen wall. "We just need to wait him out."

"Or Mom could go to Hudson's? If she wraps a scarf around her head and uses my car, the police can follow her instead," Raina said. It would be safe enough if her mom went straight to her boyfriend's house.

"You know this trick will only work once, right?" Po Po asked.

"It's a bad idea," Mom said. She yawned, exposing her silver fillings. "I had a late night."

Raina handed her a mug of coffee but ignored her comment. She addressed her grandma. "Who said anything about coming back? We could crash at Cassie's tonight, and this would give you an opportunity to put the screws on Benson. I'm sure there's something he could tell us about the journal."

"No one would be happy with this plan," Po Po said with an impish smile on her face. "I think it's brilliant."

"What journal?" Mom asked.

"Don't worry about it, Melody," Po Po said.

Thirty minutes later, Mom plodded with her head down the two blocks toward Raina's car. She was unhappy about the situation, but she knew which side of the rice bowl she needed to be at. Raina watched the black Fiat pull away from the curb and into traffic. Sure enough, he followed Mom until both vehicles disappeared from sight.

Raina high-fived Po Po and opened the front door. A familiar unmarked vehicle turned into view. Smith! She stepped back inside the house and shut the door.

"I thought we were leaving," Po Po said.

"Change in plan," Raina said, strolling over to the big picture window. She peered through the curtains in time to see Smith pulling into a parking spot. "We'll have to leave from the back."

As they headed out the back door, they could hear the doorbell ringing. Po Po's canteen got stuck on the fence while she slid into Mr. Clark's backyard and she left it there like a calling card.

"He will have a cow when he sees the canteen," Po Po said smugly.

Raina ignored the comment and hustled them onto the Muni for Chinatown. As the bus rounded the corner, she could see Smith peering inside the bay window. She had no idea what Smith wanted, but she figured it was best to avoid any interview with the SFPD until they figured out what was going on.

She didn't want to worry her grandma with her concerns for the man who followed her mom. An unknown player in this game of cat and mouse couldn't be a good thing.

THE LINE for the Golden Gate Bakery wrapped around the block, blocking the entrance to the herbalist shop. Faded red lettering with missing letters on the dirty yellow awning read "Gol Y k Cho." The establishment might have been in business for the last fifty years, but like most

Chinese businesses, the owners sure didn't spend money on upgrades from what Raina could see on the outside.

Po Po surveyed the line with a frown. "Why don't I get in line to get us some dan tats? You go talk to the herbalist without me."

"We just had breakfast," Raina said.

"But it's my favorite egg tart."

"You had a box yesterday. Besides, I want you to do the talking."

"Why? Because I'm old? I'll have you know, I'm only sixty-five years old."

"Yes, I know. And tomorrow, you'll be fifty. It's not your age I need, but your smooth Chinese kinship voice. Call the owner big brother, say Martin recommended the shop, and ask for what they normally give Martin."

Po Po looked longingly at the people coming out of the bakery with their pink boxes of goodies. "How do you know the owner isn't younger than me? I don't want to go in there. The smell reminds me of my grandmother and her smelly Chinese medicine. I didn't go across an ocean just to go backward."

As the youngest daughter of the third wife, whose father went on to have a fourth wife and finally had the much-longed-for son, Po Po's childhood wavered between snubbed and forgotten. She couldn't shake the dust of China from her shoes fast enough.

"Po Po, you could sell water to a fish. That's how good you are. Now go find out the ingredients for the sleeping draughts Uncle Martin took each night," Raina said.

At their entrance, the strand of ancient Chinese coins above the door chimed. Sure enough, the shop had a blend of dried herbs and musty dead animals. Not appetizing, but they weren't here for a meal.

A young man about Raina's age glanced up from behind the counter. "How may I help you?"

"We're here to talk to the herbalist," Po Po said.

"Herb Wang, at your service. Yes, I know, my dad had a sense of humor."

Raina snorted. "Our fathers must be related. I'm Raina Sun. My brother is Winter Sun, and my sis—"

"Where's your father?" Po Po cut in. "You're too young."

"I studied under my father's tutelage for decades and graduated from Xuzhou University with a degree in traditional Chinese medicine," Herb said good-naturedly as if he had to recite his credentials regularly. "Ma'am, how may I help you?"

"First, I'm not a ma'am. That would be my grandmother. Second, I would still like to speak with your father."

"If you wish, but you'll have to come back in a month. He is touring our suppliers' facilities in China."

"Then who is seeing to your patients in the meantime?"

"Ma'am, I am."

Raina could see the steam rising from Po Po's head. "Herb, maybe you could help us," she cut in before her grandma had a chance to insult the herbalist. "We're family friends of Martin Eng's. I know he had been a patient here for many decades."

Herb's smile disappeared. "I'm sorry to read about his death on Facebook. Maybe I'm just old-fashioned, but I can't believe his family would choose to announce his death this way."

"That would be Mrs. Keane, his next-door neighbor," Po Po said. "Apparently the lady is under the delusion that she is his surviving widow."

Herb cleared his throat. "Are you here to settle his tab?" He pulled a box from underneath the counter and started to rifle through the folders. "Normally, we don't extend credit to our patients, but Mr. Eng had been with us for decades." He pulled a sheet out and slid it across the counter. "The total is one hundred fifty dollars. This is already pro-rated for the month."

So much for patient confidentiality. Raina leaned forward to study the paper. The six line items all listed "Sleeping Draught #6" in the product description. "So Uncle Martin spent seven hundred and fifty dollars each month for his sleeping draughts?" Geez, she was in the wrong profession.

Herb shrugged. "Supply and demand. It works, and he was willing to pay."

"What's in it? Crack?" Po Po asked.

"That would be privileged information." He tapped on the bill. "Cash or credit card? We don't take personal checks."

"Is there any possibility Uncle Martin might have overdosed on your herbal teas?" Raina asked.

"No."

"How can you be so sure? Every medication has a potential side effects warning label," Po Po said. "Don't you know anything about drug interaction?"

"You're not here to pay his bill," Herb said, finally

catching on. He snatched the paper from the counter. "I can't discuss my patient's treatment plan with you."

"You worry about confidentiality now?" Po Po asked.

Herb stiffened and his voice became terse. "I need to get back to my inventorying."

"Okay. Thank you for your time," Raina said. Po Po opened her mouth, but Raina continued, "I'm sure the police would love to know Uncle Martin took a sleeping draught every night. This isn't exactly something that would show up on a medical record from his doctor." She turned and walked to the shop door without waiting for her grandmother.

As she reached for the handle, Herb called out, "Wait!"

Bingo!

Raina pivoted slowly. "Yes?"

Herb's eyes narrowed as he studied her. "Why would the police be interested in his herbal supplement?"

"The man died in his sleep. Of course, the police will check to make sure there was no foul play or an overdose."

He stared at her for another long moment. His jaw clenched and unclenched as he worked through his decision. "I swear if this gets out, I will find you."

"Your secret is safe with me," Raina said.

Po Po crossed her heart and leaned forward with an eager expression.

"Sleeping Draught #6 is nothing more than the Sleepy Time tea they sell at the supermarket. We make our own blend with the same ingredients and add a drop of peppermint oil."

The silence that greeted his confession was deafening.

"Well, I guess you're lucky someone hasn't complained to the authorities about your snake oil business practices," Raina said, turning to leave. The possibility of foul play was getting stronger by the minute.

8

BITE ME

Afterwards, they had a late lunch and walked over to Joley Mok's shop. The shop was closed, so they went next door and waited for Uncle Martin's business rival to return. The milk tea shop was crowded—gyrating teenyboppers, bright lights, and loud music.

Po Po did a little jig while they waited for their drinks. "Gosh, I love this place. It's like a club for teens."

Raina grabbed their snacks and drinks and headed for a table by the window. Three teens gathered their belongings and squeezed into an already full table.

"Wow, thanks," Po Po said, flapping her hands. "Those kids are polite."

Or they didn't want to sit by a granny in pink camouflage with a pimp cane. Raina glanced at the speakers next to them. Or it could be the noise.

She slurped on her Thai iced tea with honey tapioca balls. Yum. Just the way she liked it—chewy tapioca balls with a hint of sweetness in a caffeinated iced drink. While the milk tea shops were all over the place in the Bay Area, there weren't any in Gold Springs. "What was Ah Gong doing in China in nineteen sixty-two?"

Po Po held a hand to her ear. "What?"

Raina shouted the question.

"...prove...Tai Gong..." Po Po said.

"What?"

Po Po stood, gesturing for them to go outside. As soon as they closed the shop door, Raina realized her ears were ringing.

"I said he was trying to prove himself to your Tai Gong," Po Po shouted.

"Whoa, I can hear you perfectly fine now."

"Sorry."

"You were telling me about Tai Gong?"

Her grandparents immigrated to the U.S. to start their married life with the clothes on their back. No one knew the details of the rift with the Hong Kong branch of the family. Raina didn't even know her great-grandfather's name; everyone in the family used his formal title—Tai Gong.

"Your great-grandfather believed a stronger China was better for all Chinese people, even those of us not living in the mainland," Po Po said. "When the policies of the Great Leap Forward welcomed Western ideas and practices, Tai Gong sent his youngest son to mainland China."

"Did Ah Gong want to go? Weren't the two of you engaged?" Raina asked.

"We were, but it was a different time then. You lived under your parents' roof, so you did as you were told. Your Ah Gong didn't feel like he had a choice." Her grandma gave her a sideways glance. "Which I think is a pile of dung, but I was a rebel even then."

Raina smiled. Not only was her grandma's mother an opera singer before her elevation to third wife, she'd left her husband and opened a dance hall when the fourth wife came along. To say her grandma had unconventional ideas was an understatement. "Let me guess? It was too risky of an endeavor to send the eldest son."

Her grandma nodded in agreement. "Ah Gong was in Beijing working as an assistant to the Ministry of Agriculture due to his father's connection, but later he was sent to a remote village to check on the agricultural production. I didn't hear from him for eight months." Her voice cracked. "I never found out what happened during that time."

"Ah Gong didn't tell you?"

Po Po shook her head and pressed her lips into a thin line.

Raina wondered if she and her grandma had the same thought—did Ah Gong fall in love with someone else during those missing months? And was the affair written in the missing journal?

She called Joley Mok's office but ended up in voicemail. "I don't think we'll catch her today. Want to go see what Mrs. Keane has to say about finding Uncle Martin's body? She looks like a talker."

"And something else," Po Po mumbled under her breath.

During the bus ride, Raina texted her mom, asking for a status update. Within seconds the return message said she was at Hudson's apartment, waiting for his return from a meeting with Smith. Immediately, three more messages came from her Mom complaining about the lack of progress. Raina didn't even bother replying. She was just glad the man in the Fiat left her mom alone after he discovered the ruse.

By the time they got off the bus at the stop near Uncle Martin's house, it was close to six. The streetlight cast unreliable shadows on the uneven sidewalk in front of them. Raina held onto her grandma's elbow. The last thing she needed was for Po Po to trip and fall.

"Still afraid of the dark?" her grandma asked.

"I'm shaking in my underwear. Now we need to make this quick," Raina whispered. "It'll take us another hour to get to Cassie's from here. I would like to say good-night to Lila before the baby goes to bed."

"I wish I wore my ninja outfit."

Raina glanced at the pimp cane sticking out from her grandma's backpack. "You're fine. If you had darkened your face, you could be mistaken for Rambo in that outfit."

Po Po frowned, probably thinking about her missed opportunity.

The townhouses were dark when they arrived at the end of the street. Most of the residents were probably stuck in traffic, trying to get home. Mrs. Keane's unit had a light on in the back of the house. The bright headlights of an approaching car spotlighted them for an instant before the driver passed them to pull into a parking spot on the curb.

Raina grabbed her grandma, dragging her through the gate of the townhouse two doors away from Uncle Martin's home. She ducked down behind the hedges.

"What—"

"Shush," Raina hissed. "That's Smith's car."

A door slammed and footsteps headed toward their direction. Raina dropped into a crouch, pulling her grandma down next to her. The porch light didn't penetrate their hiding spot, but she felt exposed all the same with their backs facing the open windows of the house behind them. If someone looked out, they were toast.

She peered through the vegetation in time to see Smith enter Uncle Martin's townhouse. Great. Who knew how long he would be there? As she debated whether to wait for the detective out or leave, another car turned into the block. The driver parked on the driveway and headed up the stairs. As he passed under a porch light, Raina gasped at the potbelly on the man.

"What is Hudson doing here?" Po Po whispered.

Raina held out her palm. "Where's your super stink bomb?"

Po Po pulled out a snack-size Tupperware container from her backpack and took off the plastic lid. The tiny glass vials twinkled when they caught the streetlight. So innocent and so deadly. "How are you going to throw it into the house without being seen?"

Raina sometimes wondered if her grandma could read her mind. She would have to force Smith and Hudson out of the townhouse. "Wait for me here. Stay hidden." She grabbed a handful and shoved them into her pocket.

As she trotted toward Uncle Martin's unit, she pulled up the collar of her jacket and kept her face down. Another busy city person on a mission to go home. In front of Uncle Martin's home, she tied her shoelaces, scanning the surrounding area. No shadows in the windows. Good.

She took one deep breath and raced up the stairs in one smooth motion. Flipping the mail slot open on the front door, she tossed the handful of stink bombs onto the tile entryway.

Clink, clink, clink.

The breaking glass was music to her ears. But there wasn't any time to enjoy the trick. Time to get out of here before the men rushed out from the home.

Raina threw one leg over the rail and launched across the three feet into Mrs. Keane's front yard. She landed in the raised beds of the dead vegetable garden. Something wet and squishy spread across her bottom. She scrambled up and dropped flat on the ground next to a planter, hoping the two-foot height would hide her in the dark.

The door flung open, and Smith bolted onto the sidewalk, his face twisted into a grimace. Hudson trailed after him, coughing with tears streaming down his face. Several more seconds passed while the men coughed and spat onto the sidewalk.

Raina pressed her lips together to keep from laughing out loud. She knew all too well how it felt. The rank skunk oil filled up a person's throat and burned through the membranes in the nostrils as if the funk were trying to imprint itself on the brain. She'd forbade Po Po from bringing the stink bombs into her apartment after the incident last Christmas.

Smith cleared his throat. "What the heck happened? Is there another dead body in there?"

Hudson stiffened as if insulted. "What do you need me to identify? I don't have all night."

Smith pulled out a faded brown leather journal with the Chinese longevity character in gold lettering.

Raina's eyes widened. This was the last place she'd expected Ah Gong's journal to show up. How did it end up with Smith?

"Recognize this? It doesn't appear to be in your uncle's handwriting," Smith said.

Hudson held out his hand. "What is it?"

"Did you know Martin Eng practiced cannibalism in China during the 1960s?" Smith ran his fingers along the edge, fanning the pages. "Martin even tried to eat the previous Dai Lo from the Nine Dragons when he was still a boy in China."

Raina's hands tightened around the leafy plant in front of her, crushing the leaves until it was a pulpy mess. This couldn't be happening. Ah Gong saved the grandfather of Sonny Kwan, the new triad boss? How could her grandfather be BFF with someone like Martin Eng?

Hudson's expression didn't change, but his body vibrated with suppressed energy. He stiffened and stared down his nose at the shorter detective. "Who have you been talking to? That's libel."

Smith raised an eyebrow as if confused at the reaction. "It's all written here. I have no idea who this belongs to, but there are sufficient details for me to know it's not a work of fiction. Apparently the owner of this journal saved the Dai Lo. Interesting stuff. Better than any book I've read lately."

Hudson glared at the detective. "My uncle was an upstanding citizen in the community. I'll sue the SFPD for ruining his reputation if these lies get out."

"What about Dai Lo? He had a good reason to hold a grudge against the man who tried to eat him as a child."

"Shame on you. My uncle's cold body is still at the morgue, and here you are spreading vicious rumors about the dead."

A car turned onto the street. Its headlight flashed across the two men on the sidewalk. Raina shifted, wiggling her toes and hoping to keep the pins and needles sensation at bay.

Hudson took a deep breath, forcing himself to relax. He jammed his fisted hands into the pockets of his jacket. "Is this all you need, Detective? My fiancée is waiting to have dinner with me."

When did he propose to her mom? Did this mean Raina no longer had to investigate Uncle Martin's death?

"Thank you for indulging me, Mr. Rice. Don't plan on leaving town." Smith crossed the street and got into his car.

Hudson watched as the detective pulled into traffic, his face hidden by the shadows. After several seconds he locked up the front door of the townhouse and left in his car, unaware of his audience.

By the time Raina got her stiffened body to move back onto the sidewalk, the lights for Mrs. Keane's place were dark. What an early sleeper. And snooping in Uncle Martin's home wasn't an option; it needed a good airing from the rancid odor seeping out from around the front door.

As Raina headed toward the bus stop, she huddled against the chill.

"We need to get Ah Gong's journal back," Po Po said, breaking the silence.

"Are you suggesting we break into the evidence room of the police station?" Raina asked.

"No, of course not, but there has to be a way. I wonder how Smith ended up with the journal?"

Raina tilted her head, trying to recall what had occurred on the day she and Smith chased after Scar Face outside of Uncle Martin's house. By the time she had gotten to the intersection, Smith shoved his hands into his jacket pocket. Could it be possible the journal fell out of Scar Face's pocket when he ran away from them? It was a stretch, but all she had at the moment.

She told her grandma the theory. "Do you believe Uncle Martin practiced cannibalism?" Did Ah Gong participate as well? Was this the reason he never talked about his mission to mainland China?

How did it relate to the secret wife and child Ah Gong wanted to take care of with the three million dollars he left for them via Raina?

Po Po didn't answer. She didn't need to.

Raina was sure both of them were thinking about Ah Gong's journal and the answers it might hold. And now that Smith had the book, all she had to do was get the journal from the SFPD. Easy peasy. Simple as baking a cake.

9

EVERY SHADE OF UGLY

It was a little after eight when they showed up at Cassie's front door in Daly City. She didn't seem happy to see them, but ushered them into the living room anyway. "Is something wrong? Has something happened to Mom?"

"Nothing is wrong, honey," Po Po said. "We need a place to stay for the night."

Relief and confusion warred across Cassie's face. "I don't understand. Why are you here?"

"It's a long story," Raina said. Involving her sister in the investigation meant another lecture for sure. No way was she in the mood for that.

Cassie crossed her arms. "I can open a bottle of wine. It's not like I have to wake up early tomorrow morning for anything."

Raina didn't know how to interpret the comment. Though she would never voice the thought, she'd wondered if her brother-in-law's proposal to her sister was a calculated career move. Two years after the marriage, he'd made partner at their Uncle Anthony's law firm.

"Is Lila in bed already?" Po Po asked.

"An hour ago. Benson is in the office upstairs reading some legal stuff," Cassie said.

Raina's cell phone chirped. It was Blue. "Excuse me, but I need to take this. Po Po can explain everything." Hopefully her sister would dismiss half of what their grandma said, like usual.

She stepped into the kitchen and tapped her phone. "Hi, Blue."

"Are you busy?" Blue asked. His voice sounded strained.

"It's been a long day. I'm at Cassie's at the moment."

"I found out about Martin Eng's death on Facebook. I'm sorry. Is there anything I can do to help?"

She shook her head even though he couldn't see her. "No. I'm used to death and mayhem. You might not want to spend too much time with me. I have a bad habit of attracting dead bodies."

She chuckled to show she was joking. Her habit of poking her nose in other people's business might scare him off. They were still in the early stage of the relationship where she would shave her legs if she knew he was coming over.

"This isn't the right time, but do you want to have dinner tomorrow night? I want to see you again before you leave town."

She did a little jig in the kitchen, but her voice sounded casual. "I might stick around for a few more days."

"But what about your classes? Or work?"

She could hear the smile in his voice. "The people here need me. The professors would understand since Uncle Martin is almost family. And I'm sure my co-workers wouldn't mind picking up extra hours since midterms are over."

They chatted for a few more minutes and said their goodbyes. She leaned her elbows on the kitchen table, wondering when she should tell Blue about her hobby. Or if she even needed to disclose this information? Most people didn't air their dirty underwear this early in a relationship, so she might be over-thinking this whole thing. She should just have a night on the town and enjoy herself.

She called Eden, but her best friend didn't pick up, so she left a message about needing to talk about Blue. It wasn't until she hung up when she realized her message sounded pathetic. She finally had a nice man in her life and here she was, whining over whether or not she was ready to commit. Sometimes she should walk into a wall to knock some sense into herself.

Then she called the Victorian but ended up with voicemail. She didn't expect her mother to be home, but she had hoped Win would work on his homework. She called her Mom's cell phone.

"Did you find anything out today?" Mom asked.

"Where are you?" Raina asked.

"At Hudson's. Did you find out anything today?"

"Where's Win? It's a school night. Shouldn't he be home?"

There was a pause. "I think he's spending the night at a friend's house."

Raina ground her teeth.

"I'm giving Win his freedom. He'll be on his own at college next year. This is good practice for him."

Raina said nothing. She wasn't going down this road. It wasn't her job to be the parent.

"If you don't have any news, I do," Mom said, not noticing the silence. "The coroner confirmed that Martin died of asphyxiation. Someone put the silk crane pillow over his face last night."

Raina gasped at the thought of the murderer killing Uncle Martin with a gift from her grandparents. Her grandma would flip when she found out the silk pillow she'd brought from Japan ended up as the murder weapon.

"Will you calm down? It's not like Martin is really your uncle." Mom sounded a little annoyed as if she didn't like being upstaged. "She also requested additional lab work, so I wonder if he overdosed himself with his sleeping draught. You know how unreliable the dosage for herbal teas can be."

"Who did you have to bribe to get this information about the lab work and the pillow?" There was no way Smith would share this information with her mom like they were schoolgirls having a chat.

Mom grew coy. "I have my sources. Now what did you find out today?"

"The sleeping draught is just overpriced Sleepy Time tea." She summarized her interview with the herbalist.

"Is this all you found out today?"

Raina took a deep breath. She needed to stay calm or she might say something she'd regret later, especially since her relationship with her mom was precarious. She could tell her mom about Ah Gong's journal, but this would lead into a lengthy explanation about the secret family. Po Po should be the one to break this news to the rest of the family. "Mom, does he make you happy?"

"Yes, I haven't felt this way since your father was alive."

"I'm glad you're happy. I'll do my best to help sort this out for Hudson."

"Of course you will, sweetie. I can always count on you to do what needs to be done. Good night, baby."

Raina blinked rapidly at the burning tears behind her eyes. She was too old to be seeking her mother's approval, but it felt good to hear it all the same. If only she could hold on to this moment a while longer.

When she returned to the living room, she found Po Po asleep on the sofa with a blanket thrown over her. Cassie had gone to bed without even saying good night.

By the time Raina woke up the next morning, everyone already had breakfast and Benson had long since left for work. She shuffled down the stairs. Her backside felt like someone had stretched her over a rack overnight. So jumping into Mrs. Keane's front yard wasn't the smartest move, but she now knew the location of the journal.

She poured herself a cup of coffee and strolled into the living room. The scene that greeted her could be cozy —Po Po and Cassie chatted while Lila pushed a toy car in front of them on the floor—except for the white-knuckle grip her sister had around her mug. If she were holding a wineglass, she would have snapped the stem in two.

Raina returned to the kitchen for a bowl of cereal, not wanting to interrupt the discussion. Her sister wouldn't thank her for getting involved. There was no point in hanging around here with her brother-in-law in the office. She would have to make a trip to the law office after she picked up her car. She texted her mom asking for the status of her car and got a reply that it was at the Victorian.

As she spooned another bite of Honey Nut Cheerios into her mouth, she grabbed the notepad next to the phone and scribbled down her notes. She needed a game plan if she were to stay out of Smith's hair. She read over the list of people she needed to talk to.

BRANDI RICE, NIECE, LEFT OFF WILL.

JOLEY MOK, BUSINESS RIVAL.

MRS. KEANE, NEXT-DOOR NEIGHBOR

DAI LO? REVENGE FOR ATTEMPT CANNIBALISM?

The list wasn't much, but it would give her plenty of legwork. Since the Financial District was next to China-town, she might as well make another trip there to see if she could catch Joley Mok today.

By the time Po Po and Cassie came into the kitchen, Raina was ready to hit the road. "Mom dropped the car off this morning."

"Good. I need a bath and clean underwear. In an emergency situation, I wouldn't want to embarrass myself when a hunky man carries me out. I think this calls for a red thong," Po Po said.

"I think no one would look at your underwear when you're slung across a pair of shoulders like a bag of rice," Cassie said.

"Now I have the image of a bag of rice in a red thong." Raina covered her eyes mockingly. "Let's roll. It'll take us forty-five minutes to get across town on public trans-portation."

"I can drop you off," Cassie said. "We can leave Lila with the nanny."

Raina shared a look with her grandma. "That would be great."

~

As Cassie and Po Po drove off, Raina hopped into her car and headed for the Financial District. She was flying solo for this interview with her brother-in-law since Po Po preferred shopping at Union Square with her sister. If Raina had a choice, she'd rather pick bellybutton lint than have this upcoming conversation.

She pulled into the underground parking, knowing full well it would cost her ten dollars an hour with validation, but for once she didn't care. Trying to find out how Ah Gong had gained his secret family fell in the upkeep category as far as she was concerned, which meant the inheritance was picking up the tab.

The receptionist who had worked for her uncle for the last twenty years smiled at Raina's entrance into the office. "Your uncle is with a client right now." She glanced at her computer monitor. "He will not have time for lunch until one o'clock today."

"I'll have to catch my uncle on another day. I'm actually looking for Benson," Raina said.

While the receptionist called Benson's phone number, Raina glanced around the tastefully decorated waiting area. One summer working as an intern in this office was enough to convince her she wasn't meant to be a lawyer. But it sure was nice to have one on her speed dial.

Benson Lang strolled up to the receptionist's desk with a practiced casualness. His suit was an impeccable gray pinstripe and his full black hair was sprayed to an *au naturel* perfection. For someone in his late thirties, he didn't even have a single line of crow's feet. And since every shade of ugly could be found in his family, he must spend an extraordinary amount of time primping in front of a mirror. Unlike Raina, her brother-in-law looked like a man going places in this world.

Places that barred their door when they saw the Chinese Afro on her head or the worn T-shirts and threadbare jeans. Short of spending hours and dollars, the curly hair wasn't something she could fix. If she replaced the T-shirts and jeans with something fancier, the family might have expectations she didn't want to deal with. A graduate student who wanted to be Indiana Jones when she grew up was far simpler.

After greeting her, Benson held the door open for her. "Let's grab a coffee."

Raina followed him and mumbled a thank you. She trailed after his long strides like a child, got into the elevator making small talk about the foggy San Francisco weather, and silently brushed past the crowd to the busy café on the lobby floor.

Benson ordered for both of them, and within minutes they were sitting on patio chairs in the mezzanine with the other suited professionals. He probably thought sitting here, surrounded by outwardly successful people, reminded Raina of her "poor choice" as he once called her decision to give up her career. Sometimes she wondered if the deterioration of her relationship with Cassie started when her sister said yes to his proposal.

"Why are you limping?" Benson asked.

"Long story. I don't want to take up your billable hours with my antics."

"What is it you don't want Cassie to know? Are you in trouble with the law again?"

Raina gave her brother-in-law credit for being sharp, except he always made assumptions about her that would be disappointing if she'd cared. "Why did you tape Ah Gong's journal behind the mirror in your bedroom?"

He averted his gaze and sipped his coffee, stretching out this simple maneuver as if Raina didn't know this trick. "It's rude to go into your host's bedroom without permission."

Ah, first the chastising. "Long bathroom line. You're lucky I didn't take a shower while I was in there."

He rolled his eyes heavenward. So much for the polished lawyer. "Someday you're going to end up on the wrong side of the law."

"Then it's a good thing you're on the right side of it. About Ah Gong's journal?"

Benson leaned back on his chair. "Lawyer-client privilege."

"Is that what you want me to tell Po Po?"

He gave her a long stare. Like the rest of her cousins, Benson still held out for an inheritance from the matriarch of the family. "Your grandfather gave me the journal for safekeeping when he was at the hospital. And before you ask, I don't know what's in it."

"You don't have a gut feeling about this particular journal?"

"I was just humoring him, figuring it would help us when he divided up his assets." He gave Raina a pointed look. "Apparently it didn't help at all since Cassie got one dollar like the rest of the cousins."

Raina returned his stare. Her brother-in-law had conveniently forgotten that Ah Gong had set aside money to pay for his daughter's college education.

He glanced at his Cartier watch and stood. "I have to go."

"Wait! You didn't even peek inside? Read a few entries?" Even a saint would be curious.

Benson gave her a mortally offended look. "No, I didn't 'peek inside.' Your grandfather tricked me into taking twenty-five cents as a retainer."

After her pointless interview with her brother-in-law, Raina called her grandma to say she was heading to Chinatown. Po Po asked to be picked up, and Raina circled the Macy's block three times and made an illegal park to load her grandma and her gazillion shopping bags. At least the short drive to Chinatown had no traffic.

Joley Mok's office was in a nondescript brick building, where the main floor storefront was a grocery store that spilled onto the sidewalk. An ADA inspector would have a field day at the place, but then he would have the same fun at every other store in Chinatown.

They rode the elevator up to the eighth floor. The door opened to a mezzanine full of daylight from solar tubes and potted greenery. The wall on the left featured a small waterfall tumbling over rocks and into an indoor pool with splashing Koi fishes. There was wicker furniture underneath a trellis covered with ivy. Strategically scattered throughout the mezzanine were charms such as ancient coins, knots made of red silk, and other paraphernalia of the feng shui trade.

Joley Mok must have rice, as the Chinese saying went, to be able to afford the entire eighth floor. Eight was the most sought after number in the community because it was a homonym to wealth. Chinese businesses would go through extreme lengths to have the number on their address or phone number.

Raina paused at the lettering on the glass door.

JOLEY MOK, PRIVATE INVESTIGATOR AND FENG SHUI MASTER

A dick and a ghost whisperer? Now that wasn't a combo a person saw every day.

10

PLAYING WITH DRAGONS

Raina suppressed a tingle of anticipation. Could this be the pay dirt she had been waiting for? If nothing else, Joley could strengthen her prayers to her ancestors to help her find her grandfather's journal.

Underneath the trellis and through another glass door was an office. A giant man of Mongol descent sat behind an old desk, using a traditional brush to paint red Chinese calligraphy on yellow tissue paper. The red ink formed characters for peace, health, and prosperity. A prayer or ritual would fuse these words into charms. She'd carried a peace charm in her wallet since her teens.

At their approaching footsteps, he glanced up. His face broke into a wide smile and he came around the table. He was tall, almost six and a half feet, probably in his early fifties. His nose was the most prominent feature on his face, a bulb that made his narrow eyes appear as slits when he smiled.

Po Po held out her hands for a hug, and the man

wrapped his beefy arms around her. Her grandma disappeared into the hug like Cheerios sucked into a vacuum.

The giant broke the hug, laughing as he patted Po Po's shoulders. "Here for a visit, Bonnie?"

"No, Ralf. We're here to consult with Joley," Po Po said. "This is my granddaughter, Raina Sun."

As she shook his hand, she gave her grandma a sideways glance. Her grandma appeared to know Ralf and Joley. Did this have something to do with what she found so upsetting at Martin's house prior to his death?

"Why don't you wait outside? I'll make us a pot of tea and get Joley." He disappeared behind the beaded curtain next to the desk.

Raina wandered over to the pond. She grabbed a handful of fish food from the small tub on the ledge and tossed it in the water. It rippled into a blur of flashing tails and opened mouths. She sighed as the tension drained from her body.

"This is the beauty of feng shui. When everything is in balance, you feel better without knowing the source," a melodic voice said.

Raina glanced up from the soothing water. A Chinese woman approached her in bell-bottom jeans and a wine-colored cardigan. Her face was smooth and luminous. They looked to be about the same age, but the other woman's eyes spoke of hidden depths. Raina felt dowdy and unsophisticated even though she couldn't explain why if anyone had asked.

The other woman held out her hand. "Joley Mok."

Raina shook her hand, and a jolt of energy surged through her. She snatched her hand back, flushing at her reaction. What was that?

Joley's lips curled as if holding back a smile. Her bottomless eyes studied Raina as if she were an interesting puzzle. "Let me guess—I'm younger than you expected."

"No, your soul is even older than my grandma's." Raina's eyes widened as the words left her mouth. *Now, where did that come from?*

Joley laughed, a tinkling like running water in a copper flume. "You are more astute than you think." She led the way back to the wicker chairs underneath the trellis.

While they distributed the teacups and almond cookies, Po Po chatted with Ralf about Uncle Anthony of all things. After everyone had a taste, Po Po told the duo about Martin Eng's death. "According to the nephew, the two of you argued publicly about your credentials, which led to several canceled bookings." She looked around, then returned her gaze to the pair. "I don't remember you having the entire floor to yourself the last time I was here."

Ralf chuckled into his teacup. When Joley shot him a look, he crammed a cookie into his mouth. He was old enough to be Joley's father, but it was clear she was in charge.

"I'm sorry about Martin Eng's death. I don't understand why Hudson immediately thought there was foul play," Joley asked. "And canceled bookings are just the nature of this business. People have faith until things get better."

"Feng shui is serious business. No self-respecting Chinese family will trust their luck and prosperity on someone who is only half Chinese," Ralf said.

And hence the motive to finish Martin off, thought Raina. "Aren't you upset with being called a fraud in front of clients?"

Joley shook her head. "I've been called worse. Feng shui is a small component of what I do for a living. So even if I lose all my clients tomorrow, I would still be okay."

"Why are you here? As much as I like to visit with friends, you're not the type to sit and chat," Ralf said to Po Po.

"I need your help. Someone has been watching the house, and I suspect it's the Nine Dragons," Po Po said.

Raina gasped. What the—

"Did you think the SFPD would have the manpower to put us under surveillance without cause?" Po Po asked, looking straight at her. She returned her attention to Joley and Ralf. "The Nine Dragons had left our family alone for decades. I want to know why they are following my granddaughter now, and what was Martin doing with Sonny Kwan's phone number?"

Raina inhaled sharply, her nostrils flaring. Her heart rate raced as fear shot through her. Everyone knew the Nine Dragons was the Chinese version of the Sopranos. Why would they be interested in her?

Joley and Ralf glanced at each other, sharing an entire conversation with this one look. "Wrangling with gangsters isn't our usual line of business—"

"Why do you think it's me?" Raina's voice squeaked, not that she wanted the triad to be interested in anyone else in her family.

"The Fiat followed your car yesterday. If someone was

following your mom, she would have freaked out by now," Po Po said. "I'm sorry, Rainy, but it had to be you."

"It must be Ah Gong's journal," Raina whispered, giving herself a mental slap on the forehead. "Everything was fine until I flashed the book around at Lila's party." She was an idiot.

"Don't be so hard on yourself," Ralf said.

Raina flashed a smile at the giant. No wonder Po Po liked this guy.

"Sonny Kwan became Dai Lo when his grandfather went into hiding. He's on shaky ground in the organization. It's a matter of time before someone challenges him for the title," Joley said. "Maybe he didn't want his old family secrets to come out."

"I don't see what this has to do with our family," Raina said. Was Joley pointing fingers at the Nine Dragons to camouflage her own motives?

"Sonny's grandfather, Ah Gong, and Martin were in the same village in China in nineteen sixty-two," Po Po said.

"Could Ah Gong have documented something the Chinese government wanted hidden?" Not that Raina believed the journal was central to a government conspiracy, but the question had to be asked.

Joley frowned, wrinkling her brow. "As I recall, the Great Leap Forward was an absolute disaster which led to the starvation of millions of people and widespread cannibalism in the countryside. China exported grain to Africa because the head didn't know what the tail was doing."

"If there wasn't enough food for its own people, why

would the government feed another country?" Raina asked.

"The government implemented Western agricultural practices that weren't applicable to an undeveloped country. The local party boss would rather report a yield three to four times more than to admit failure. So to the paper pushers in Beijing, the country had plenty of food," Joley said.

Raina nodded, recalling her conversation with Martin the night before his death. The elders came up with the idea to transplant seedlings from all the nearby fields into the one field the government officials came to inspect. No wonder the government thought there was plenty of food.

"So Ah Gong witnessed some of the atrocities during his short stint in the countryside. How is this relevant today?" Po Po asked.

Raina glanced at Joley, noting the professionally blank expression on her face. What if her grandfather did more than just witness? Look at what happened during Katrina. People did unspeakable things to each other when order broke down. And hunger in the middle of winter was the fastest route to chaos. There was a reason Ah Gong never spoke of that time in his life.

And what would the Nine Dragons do to bury the shameful secrets of its founding Dai Lo? History had a way of becoming relevant today in ways that were stranger than fiction.

"I need to sleep on your request for help with the Nine Dragons," Joley said, standing to indicate their interview was over.

Raina glanced at her grandma, who was busy gathering her backpack and cane. "Are you interested in getting rid of Weeping May?" Raina asked. This would give her another opportunity to see if Joley was good at her craft. This prosperous business owner image could be nothing more than a mirage.

Po Po explained the situation with Weeping May haunting the old Victorian.

Joley looked amused as if she knew Raina's reason for suggesting the booking. "Sure, I can come by and have a look."

They left the building and went into a hot pot restaurant two blocks away for dinner. Raina missed having decent restaurants within sneezing distance from each other when she was in Gold Springs.

The restaurant was crowded. The steam from the boiling soup base filled the windows with condensation. Hot pot was a meal made for those who didn't mind having raccoon eyes from smeared mascara. It wasn't a place for a first date.

Po Po slurped the soup base in the ladle. "Oh, this is good. Just the right kick of hot and spicy." She dumped several raw slices of beef flank into the soup.

Raina's mouth watered at the full-bodied soup, but she ignored it. "How come you didn't mention our family's connection to the Nine Dragons before today?"

"Honey, you will give me indigestion with your questions. Can't we eat first?"

"I already have indigestion thinking about you wrangling with the triad."

Po Po paused, soup ladle suspended in midair. Her smile grew wider as the thoughts flew across her face. "Hmmm...I haven't mud wrestled in years."

"What else do you know about the Nine Dragons? Not having this information could get me killed."

"If you must insist on ruining this meal..." Po Po placed the ladle on the table and folded her hands in front of her like a student ready for a recital. "There's no need to talk about killings. Our family's shipping business was one of the few who never paid protection money to the Nine Dragons."

"Does Ah Gong have something on the triad?"

"I'm not sure. In those days, a wife didn't question her husband like she would now. It just wasn't done."

"There's what's not done and what you did behind the scenes. You're not the type to stand in the corner studying your toe jam."

"Your grandfather could have cashed in a chip with the previous Dai Lo during a hostile takeover which fell through in the seventies."

"If Martin called Scar Face—"

"Who?"

"The guy who mugged me at the BART station. Someone at the party must have called him about the journal."

"But why would Martin call him? If there were any truth to the cannibalism theory, wouldn't he avoid the Nine Dragons altogether?"

"Ah Gong and Martin were BFFs. If Ah Gong had something on the previous Dai Lo, this could be why they left Martin alone until now."

Po Po held out a wonton on her chopstick, and Raina shook her head. "Their relationship was antagonistic enough for family. Martin got into this country as Ah Gong's paper brother. But towards the end, they weren't friends anymore. At the time, I thought it was the medication Ah Gong was taking, but now I'm not so sure."

Decades ago, some families brought over paper relatives to the United States in exchange for money. Officially, they were related to the sponsor, but in reality, the paper relative might have been a friend or even a stranger.

Raina blotted the sweat on her upper lip. The spices and steam from the boiling soup could clear a person's sinuses. "Why did Ah Gong bring him to the U.S. if they weren't friends? And why did we still welcome the Eng family to parties and such?"

"Old habits, I guess. It wasn't until years later after Martin divorced my cousin I found this out."

Her head ached at the complications between the three men who were at the same remote village in China during the sixties. Martin had something on Ah Gong, and her grandfather had something on the previous Dai Lo, which resulted in a ceasefire between the previous Dai Lo and Martin. She told her grandma her theory. "With Ah Gong's death, Martin lost his protection. So the killer could be an assassin from the triad."

"The only thing Martin might have on Ah Gong is information about the other woman," Po Po said, her voice clogged with suppressed tears. "Once our children got old enough, I went with Ah Gong to China for every business trip. I knew all about businessmen and their other wives. Look at my father and his four wives." She shook her head. "I left my poor babies to fend for themselves with Tai Ma, and he still ended up with another wife and son."

"Great-grandma did a good job taking care of them, so don't beat yourself up." Raina patted her grandma's hand. "I know just the thing to cheer you up. After we finish here, we should take a look-see at Martin's townhouse. We might as well put your disguise to use." Today her grandma had on gray camo.

Po Po attempted to smile, but it didn't erase the forlorn expression in her eyes.

She knew how her grandma felt. This fiasco with this other family was the reason she'd stopped believing in ever after. Fairy tales existed for other people. "We made good progress today." She pulled the notebook she'd snagged from her sister out of her purse. "Let me update my suspect list and what we learned so far."

"I can't believe you're still using paper. So old-fashioned." Po Po pulled a tablet from her backpack. "We can put the list online and share it to our phones."

"We can do it your way, but I still like paper better. And what about security? We wouldn't want to accidentally post this on Facebook."

"Oh, come on. There's no such thing as accidental posting." Po Po shook her head. "Some people are just attention hogs."

Raina pretended to wipe her mouth with a napkin to hide her smile. And the kettle just called the stove black…

Her grandma's fingers flew across the keyboard on the glass screen, typing up the notes from the notepad. Raina always hated typing on a tablet.

"Anything you want to add?" Po Po asked.

"Hudson didn't notice any signs of a break-in, so the killer had to be someone Martin knew," Raina said.

"Unless there's broken glass, I doubt if either Mrs. Keane or Hudson is observant enough."

"Don't forget Gigi. The dog would have alerted Mrs. Keane, and she seems like the type to call the police if a kid skateboarded on the sidewalk."

Raina glanced at the digital display on her phone. "Is it too late to stop by Mrs. Keane's townhouse?"

"It's been two days. Her fifteen minutes on the Internet is done. I'm sure she's dying for more attention by now." Po Po threw down her napkin. "Let's bounce."

11

A CHAT WITH NAPOLEON

As they made their way up the stoop, Gigi yipped as if she knew Raina was nearby. She pushed the buzzer for the front door, hoping the visit would be a short one. Mrs. Keane probably wouldn't be able to add more to what Hudson had already told her, but she had to check every box even though she was only pretending to be a PI.

Mrs. Keane's face appeared at the bay window and disappeared. The scratching on the other side grew more frantic and then stopped.

Raina rocked back and forth on the balls of her feet. Her gaze traveled around the neat landing area on top of the staircase. The fence-enclosed front yard raised bed planter held crushed leafy plants she couldn't identify. She winced at the damages from her ninja move last night.

Po Po leaned on the pimp cane as if she needed the support. Raina had a feeling her grandma would play the harmless old lady in this interview.

The front door clicked open and Mrs. Keane gestured for them to come inside. Gigi was nowhere in sight, but a faint yipping came from the rear of the townhouse.

In the living room, Raina sat on the edge of the over-sized sofa. The deep seat made it impossible for her to touch the backrest without resorting to hopping on the furniture. With her feet dangling above the floor, she felt like a child about to have a serious conversation with a grown-up. Her grandma jumped onto the sofa and got into the lotus position with her cane across her knees.

Mrs. Keane sat on a normal-sized armchair, calmly watching the two of them get comfortable. Without an audience, Mrs. Keane seemed almost serene even though her perm was tight as ever. Her head must ache from the strain.

The room was dim, and the single lamp lent a stillness to the room as if they were at a sleepover ready to share secrets.

"It looks like I'm still on Gigi's naughty list, huh?" Raina asked.

The faint yipping stopped for a few seconds and started up again.

"Are you wearing any kind of perfume? She's friendly with everyone else," Mrs. Keane said with pretended interest.

Raina shook her head to the perfume question. "Anyways, we want to see how you are holding up? Hudson said the two of you found Uncle Martin's body. It must be a shock."

Mrs. Keane pulled a handkerchief from her sleeve and dabbed at her eyes, which were dry as a desert. "He could have been the love of my life, but he's gone before we even started."

Raina nodded gravely. Yeah, sure. "It must be tough. How long have you been neighbors?"

"Thirty years."

"Then you must know Uncle Martin well. Did he seem different to you in the last few months? Did his routine change?"

"Not that I noticed. I didn't monitor when he came in and out."

Raina bet her last dollar Mrs. Keane was the type to glue her face to the bay window, watching the comings and goings on the street.

"Yeah, right," Po Po mumbled.

"How about other people? Have you noticed more visitors? Or have there been any changes, like someone new visiting?" Raina asked, ignoring Po Po's comment.

"Well, there's Hudson Rice. He came by regularly for the last year or so. Before that, it was his sister, Brandi, but she had a falling out with Martin. She was real friendly and appeared to treat Martin as if he were her dad. She drove him to run his errands every Sunday morning and visited with take-out food at least once a week after work. She did that for years."

"Do you know why she stopped coming by?" Po Po asked.

"I think she fell for the wrong guy and got into drugs. Martin begged her to go to rehab, said he would pay for everything, but..." Mrs. Keane shrugged. "It was too bad. She was a good girl."

"Did Martin seem to regret the fallout?" Raina asked.

"I don't know. We used to have dinner together once a

week, but he got too busy when Hudson re-appeared, passing on the family business. And then there was the diagnosis on his liver."

"Didn't he always have cirrhosis?" Po Po asked.

Mrs. Keane narrowed her eyes. She clearly didn't like losing her position as the fount of knowledge on Martin Eng. "Yes, his liver got worse in the last couple of years. More gallstones and problems with bruising. It's probably why he was in such a rush to hand over the reins to his nephew."

"Isn't it odd Martin's controlled medical condition got worse when his nephew came back into his life?" Raina didn't like to think the worst of her mother's new boyfriend, but the question had to be asked.

Mrs. Keane stared off into space for a moment. "No, I don't think so. I've seen the two of them at the health clinic a few times. Hudson was taking care of his uncle just like his sister did. Martin was lucky to have the two. I have a son, but you don't see him coming around to visit. No grandchild for me either. No woman is stupid enough to marry him. For a while, I was hoping Brandi would consent to a blind date with him."

If Brandi had hooked up with Mrs. Keane's son, would she have avoided her current boyfriend? Everything in life had to do with timing. One second too early could be one second too late.

"Anyone else visited? How about a man with a scar on his face or nunchucks?" Po Po asked, breaking into Raina's thoughts.

Mrs. Keane gaped at her grandma and shook her head. "Hudson, his girlfriend, the two of you..."

"Any late night visitors?" Raina asked.

"No…"

"Are you sure?"

"Oh, there was a Chinese woman. She left a little after eleven."

Po Po leaned forward. "A hot young girlfriend?"

"I don't know. I only saw her back. She drove off in a Mini Cooper," Mrs. Keane said.

"Did Gigi bark?" Po Po asked.

"I don't remember," Mrs. Keane said.

"So could this person be someone who has visited Martin before?" Raina asked.

Mrs. Keane shrugged. "Gigi has real good hearing, and she can smell things from a mile away. She always barks when you're around. It has to be your perfume."

Raina held out her arm. "I'm not wearing any perfume. Do you want to take a sniff?"

Mrs. Keane sniffed her hand. "Can't smell a thing. Maybe that's the problem. You're like a blank slate to a sensitive nose."

Raina's nose itched, and she had to twist away to keep from sneezing on Mrs. Keane's hair.

"Officer Smith called right before you got here. He's coming over to ask me follow-up questions." Mrs. Keane's eyes lit up like fireworks. "This is the most excitement I've had in months."

Raina shared a look with her grandma. She didn't want to be around when Smith showed up. "We should get going."

The doorbell rang.

Raina bit her lower lip to keep from cursing and ended up sneezing instead. "It's time for us to get out of your way."

They followed Mrs. Keane to the door. Mrs. Keane opened the front door to reveal Smith with his hand poised over the doorbell. "Officer Smith, did you fly over here? I wasn't expecting you for another half hour."

"Detective Smith, ma'am." He blocked the entire landing. They would have to ram into him to leave. "Miss Sun, I'm glad you're here. I have a few questions for you."

"Officer, I have to leave for my knitting club. I can't wait until you're done with Raina," Mrs. Keane said, miffed at losing the limelight.

Bang!

Raina jumped at the noise from the back of the house. Po Po swung around with her cane raised across her body. Smith swept past the women and into the house, pulling out his gun. Gigi burst into the living room and ran straight for Smith's crotch.

Mrs. Keane screamed, "No! Gigi!"

Raina covered her face.

"Sit!" Smith commanded, his voice booming out.

The Boston terrier tried to stop—her rear end dropped and front paws slid on the hardwood floors. The momentum carried her little body forward, and she barreled into Smith. Gigi lifted her head and licked his hand; then she yipped at Raina.

While Smith untangled himself from Gigi's greeting, Raina hustled her grandma out of the townhouse. Out the stoop and down the steps.

"Miss Sun, one moment please," Smith called out from behind her.

Raina wanted to scream in frustration. She felt like a child who just had her lollipop taken away after the first lick. She whirled around, hoping she didn't look guilty.

"Yes, Detective? I don't have time to talk right now. I'm running late for an appointment." She smiled at how easily the lie came to her. Practice made perfect.

Smith strutted down the stairs. The porch light lit him up like he was an actor descending upon the masses. A woman slowed her steps on the sidewalk to gawk. He didn't even notice. Raina was more impressed he could strut in the semi-darkness without falling.

Smith tossed his head and a stray lock fell across his face. "Hi, what are you doing tonight?" He ignored her grandma, who stepped away from them with a snicker.

Raina suppressed her grimace. She didn't fail to notice he remained on the last step of the stairs so he could tower over her. Napoleon complex was alive and thriving here. "I have a date."

He didn't even blink. "Tomorrow night?"

"What do you want?"

"I made a few calls to Gold Springs. You're some kind of amateur. I thought we could trade war stories over dinner."

Raina laughed, snorting in an unladylike manner. "Please don't tell me you want to team up or something."

"What if I do?"

"Seriously?" She straightened as the amusement left her. This could be the opportunity she had been waiting for. "Okay, I'll bite. I want my grandfather's journal back. I saw you picked it up when we chased the guy with the white hoodie on the day Uncle Martin died." It was worth throwing the theory on the wall to see if it stuck.

"I don't know what you're talking about." He shrugged as if what she had to say didn't matter. "This would be a great networking opportunity for you to talk to a real cop about investigating a homicide. You could tell me what you found out so far and I can give you my take on things. What do you say?"

She gave him a regretful smile as if she were dying to share her suspicions. "Maybe some other time." He must've thought she was an idiot. What cop would discuss an active case with a civilian who was linked to the victim?

He gave her a business card. "Here's my cell phone number if you change your mind."

As they walked back to her car, Raina felt his eyes on her the entire time. He wanted something from her all right, but networking wasn't one of them. Now if she could figure out what this was, then maybe she could use it as leverage to get her grandfather's journal back from the SFPD.

12

TWISTED UNDERWEAR

The next morning, the black Fiat was back on their street. Raina stepped away from the curtains when the driver got out. Scar Face! He leaned against the car and lit a cigarette.

Heart pounding, she dashed into the kitchen. "We need to leave. Scar Face is coming up to the house."

Po Po hustled to the living room but returned within seconds with disappointment written on her face. "There's no one outside."

Raina sagged against the kitchen island in relief. Where did he go? "Po Po, please drive around the block in Mom's car. I'll meet you in front of Mr. Clark's house." Better safe than sorry. The neighbor behind the Victorian would just have to deal.

Five minutes later, they were on their way to have a chat with Brandi. The address they got from Mom was located in West Oakland, a seedy part of town dominated by run-down Victorians and new condos with graffiti. Despite the chill, two scruffy-looking teenage boys played ball on a basketball court next to a sad excuse of a park—a swing set with a missing seat, sand filled with cigarette butts and bottle caps, and illegal dumping.

Raina pulled up next to the curb. The minivan in front of them bore the remains of a late night bonfire—the charred marshmallow sticks still stuck to ashes on the hood. "Let's make this fast. Could you take that hat off? We shouldn't draw more attention to ourselves."

Po Po hopped out of the vehicle, pulling the purple velvet Fedora hat lower on her head. "It's cold today." Her breaths came out in pale puffs in front of her. "Let's get this show on the road." As she strode toward the apartment building, she twirled her pimp cane, the gold horse statue glittering in the morning sun. If Raina squinted, her grandma fit right in with the neighborhood.

Through the opening, they strolled into a concrete courtyard that held two discarded sofas and several boxes. Three stories rose around them with laundry hung like Christmas ornaments on the railings above. The main windows of the apartments faced the courtyard, intensifying the spotlight effect. An overweight black woman sprawled on a sofa, watching them.

"What ya'll lookin' for?" slurred the woman. The plastic six-pack holder was missing four cans on the box next to her.

"How are you doing?" Po Po asked.

"The day's still young and I'm trying to stay out of trouble."

"What's the fun in that? Trying to find me some."

"Word."

"We don't want any trouble," Raina cut in. "We're here to visit Brandi Rice."

The woman gave her grandma a look. "Why's her underwear in a bunch?"

Raina flushed at the implication. She wasn't a party pooper.

"She doesn't wear the stuff I buy her from Victoria's Secret." Po Po held a hand against her mouth and lowered her voice. "You never know when a lacy thong might come in handy."

"Po Po!" It was one thing for her grandma to bemoan Raina's underwear choices when they were alone, but to share it with the world? She was horrified.

The woman chuckled. "Kids, they don't listen. Brandi's up there." She turned and pointed to the corner unit on the second floor behind her. "You're in luck. Her boyfriend got hauled off to jail two days ago. You wouldn't want to meet him. Even I got tired of hearin' him slap her around, and this with my daddy taking a belt on my mom when we were growing up. He was a mean drunk, you know. Then he got killed by the city bus."

"I'm sorry," Raina said automatically, her mind racing. Two nights ago was when Martin died in his townhouse.

"Nah. It was the best thing that happened to our family. Mom moved our family East to her folks with the settlement money."

"How do you know he hasn't been back since?" Po Po asked.

"All of us would have heard him. He's always doped up on somethin'. And screaming about the devil. You would have thought he's a Baptist."

"What time did the police come by?" Raina asked.

"Late. After one, I think. I had to yell at my kids the next mornin' to get up for school. Go on with you," the woman said. "I need my 'me time' before the kids get home."

While it would be a stretch, Brandi could still make it to Martin's townhouse after the police left. As they passed by the first apartment unit, a whiff of urine and burnt bacon greeted them. Raina gagged, and she breathed through her mouth on the way up.

Po Po sucked in the scent like a greedy shop vac, even pausing to puzzle out sour grease. "I want to replicate this in my ultimate stink bomb experiment."

"Keep up or I'm leaving you behind," Raina called over her shoulder. "If you duplicate this smell while I'm around, I'm getting a new sidekick."

"You can't fire me. I'm like your Q. Without my cool toys, you couldn't do your James Bond thing."

"I don't want to be James Bond. I don't have half the muscle to shoot 'em up."

"Your skinny little behind will do. Just remember it's all about the brains, not the brawn in this line of work. You handled yourself pretty well in the last few murders."

"I'm not a pro—"

The front door to Brandi's unit opened, interrupting their banter. She jerked back in surprise. As she got a look at their faces, her eyes widened in recognition. "Wong Po Po, what are you doing here?"

The lackluster blonde hair couldn't hide the black bruise with yellowing edges on her cheek. The dark shadows underneath her eyes made her appear gaunter than she was. She held onto the doorknob to prevent them from peeking inside her apartment.

"Hi, sweetie, I heard you got yourself into a spot of

trouble," Po Po said, her voice gentle. "We're here to help."

Brandi's eyes blinked rapidly and her face struggled for control. She held open the door to reveal a packed duffel bag next to her feet. "I..."

Po Po held open her arms. "Come with us, Brandi. You're safe now."

Brandi closed her eyes; the tears spilled down her cheeks. She stepped into Po Po's arms and sobbed. Raina grabbed the bag and led the way to the car.

By the time they got back to the Victorian, Brandi had calmed after her initial outburst. She still had the kicked puppy look, but at least she appeared to be alert. They sat around the kitchen island, sipping green tea and munching on dan tats. The egg tarts weren't from the Golden Gate Bakery, but according to her grandma, they would do.

"Where are you planning to go, Brandi?" Po Po asked.

"Away."

Raina studied the flaky crust on her egg tart. Was Hudson's sister skipping town before the police caught up to her?

"Do you need any money?" Po Po asked.

Brandi bit her lip and averted her gaze. "Hudson was supposed to give me money so I could leave Austin and check into a rehab center to get cleaned up."

"Hudson made it sound like you chose your boyfriend over your family. What changed your mind about leaving him?" Raina asked.

"Money. Or the lack of it. Austin is getting stressed about our financial situation." Brandi touched the black bruise on her cheek. She jerked her hand away, curling the fingers into a fist. "All those years while Hudson was in LA, I took care of Uncle Martin like he was my father. I didn't expect a big payday, but a measly five grand? You can't even hire care for this amount. You wouldn't understand, Raina, but your cousins would."

Raina blanched at the reference to the three million dollars her deceased Ah Gong had left her. Her hands trembled, so she tucked them in her armpits. So her reputation as money-grubbing granddaughter preceded her.

Brandi and Po Po continued to chatter, but Raina wasn't listening. She had to get the journal from Smith. The research she did on the Internet hadn't yielded more than what Joley Mok had told her about the Great Leap Forward in China.

Po Po went to show Brandi the converted spare bedroom in the attic. When she came back, she asked, "Are you okay?"

Raina nodded. She wasn't all right. Being the black sheep in the family was exhausting, especially when she wasn't the one with the shameful past.

"Thank you," Po Po said.

"I don't want to do this anymore. It's not fair. Let's divide the money between the cousins and just call it good," Raina said, the words tumbling over each other in her haste to get them out. "You do not understand how awful it is to have everyone in your family misjudge you."

"I do understand. I'm the love child between my father and an opera singer. The first two wives and their children hated me for what I represented. Then, when the son finally came from the fourth wife, I was ignored. I drank family politics with my mother's milk."

"Why have secrets when open communications would have resolved hurt feelings? Keeping Ah Gong's secret like this isn't helping anyone. It's his shameful past. It's not a reflection of you as a wife or mother."

"Are you prepared to rake this family through burning coals? Do you think your uncles want to know their father had another son and wife? Everything they believed to be true is a lie."

Raina pressed her lips together. So it was more convenient to blame her for influencing their dying grandfather to give her a boatload of money. She forced her voice to remain level. "What should we do with Brandi? She can't go to her apartment. The abusive boyfriend might come back." She was tired of going around in circles whenever they spoke of Ah Gong—someone's feelings always got hurt.

"Let me take care of this. You'll have to fly solo today," Po Po said, eager to leave their standstill conversation alone.

"Do you think Brandi has anything to do with Uncle Martin's death?" Raina asked.

"I can't say. For all we know, the boyfriend might have done it." Po Po had watched Brandi grow up with her children. "The girl needs help, and she needs her family. She has agreed to rehab. I'll call around to see if there's an immediate opening somewhere. I told her not to worry about the expenses."

"Okay, I'll check in with you later. I have a date with Blue this evening. So you guys are on your own for dinner."

Raina left her grandma's house with a heavy heart for a much-needed cheeseburger. Not that she was hungry, but grease, fat, and salt chased away bad juju like nothing else. If she stayed, she might end up calling Blue to hear someone say she was beautiful. And that would be a disaster because there was no such thing as happily ever after. Why had she agreed to dinner?

13

IT'S NOT YOU

It was two o'clock by the time Raina pulled out of the drive-through and into traffic. Her stomach rumbled at the grease wafting out of the take-out bag. She jammed a handful of fries into her mouth, thinking about the investigation as it stood.

Brandi Rice was too much of a wreck and from all accounts seemed to genuinely care about her uncle. This didn't take her off the suspect list, but to kill someone for five grand seemed far-fetched.

Joley Mok and Ralf turned out to be cronies of her grandma, but this alone didn't eliminate them as suspects. However, it made no sense for them to kill a business rival when they didn't appear to be hurting for clients. While they might be at the bottom of the suspect list, they were still on the list and shouldn't be ignored until they had an alibi.

And then there was the new triad boss, Sonny Kwan. She had dismissed him as a potential suspect because she didn't want to tangle with the Nine Dragons. Initially, there appeared to be no connection between the upstanding businessman and the shady triad lead. This turned out to be a false assumption.

Her eyes widened as a thought hit her, and she sucked fries down the wrong pipe. She coughed, spraying out a mouthful of potato goop across the dashboard. Her eyes filled with tears, but she ignored them and gulped down soda to clear the residual fries in her throat. Geez, she could kill herself if she wasn't careful.

At Lila's party, Raina had overheard Uncle Martin ordering liver. Had she interpreted it so it said what she wanted to hear? What if he had ordered...human liver? Could his worsening cirrhosis turned him into a desperado? What if Uncle Martin believed eating a healthy human liver would help regenerate his? He made his living helping people cope with the supernatural and superstition, so he had to be a believer on some level.

By the time Raina got home, her grandma and Brandi were nowhere in sight. She halfheartedly went through two boxes in the attic. It occurred to her that she was the only one cleaning out the Victorian for the upcoming holiday. So much for teamwork from the rest of the family.

As she got dressed for her date with Blue, her thoughts wandered back to the murder investigation. Something had to break soon because she was burning a lot of gas going back and forth all over the City. It wasn't like she could share her frustration with her boyfriend. Her ex-boyfriend would know how she felt at the moment since he was a homicide detective in Gold Springs.

She shook her head to clear his image from her mind.

She couldn't drive forward while watching the rear-view mirror. Blue was her boyfriend now, and she didn't need her ex taking up mental real estate. She might as well enjoy her evening since the investigation for Martin's murder was going nowhere.

An hour later, Raina followed the hostess across the restaurant in her lavender wool skirt with matching knee-high suede boots, she could feel eyes following her progress and wondered if her hair got messed up in the short walk from the parking spot to the building.

Blue stood at her approach and kissed her cheek in greeting. His fawn colored cashmere sweater brought out the golden flecks in his eyes, and they lit up as he gazed at her.

"Did you wait long?" she asked, sitting on the chair he had pulled out for her.

"Just got here myself. You're a busy woman. I've been hoping you could pencil me in for dinner sooner than tonight." Blue smiled to let her know he was joking. "But I will take what I can get."

He was too polite to mention her insistence they meet at the restaurant. They both knew it was a step back in their fragile relationship. How could she explain that being in the City always made her fall into old roles in her family, which wasn't conducive to any healthy relationship? Maybe she should suggest they spend some time away from the crazies.

"Sorry, but I have to work through a few things at home." He didn't need to know about this hobby of hers until they got more serious. Most people wouldn't find tracking down killers to be a cute distraction. She needed to play it cool, so she didn't scare this nice guy away.

Blue smiled, pretending like he understood, but she knew he didn't. With no siblings and a mom he saw once a year during a holiday, he was both attracted and repelled by her large extended family.

"I'm bidding on a job at Gold Springs," he said. "Renovating an old resort for student housing. It's a big job, but I would get to spend six months in the same town with you."

She grinned toothily, both surprised and pleased. Was he hinting he would like to take their relationship to the next level? Why didn't she put on the fancy underwear—

"Are you ready to order?" the server asked, gliding to their table.

Raina gestured for Blue to go first. She flipped through the menu, heading straight for the salads. After the greasy burger this afternoon, she was ready for lighter fare. As she glanced up, a flash of silvery blond hair caught her eye.

Seated at the next table, behind Blue, was Smith. He raised his glass of red wine in silent salute to her. And to his right, at another table all by his lonesome self, was Ralf. They both smiled at her, unaware of the other's presence.

Raina's heart sped up at the thought of her two worlds colliding—amateur sleuth and girlfriend. Was this the sign she had been waiting for to let Blue in on her secret—her nosy superpower?

"Are you ready, ma'am?" the server asked.

Raina held the menu up to keep from looking at the two men watching her like she was on a dating reality show. What were they doing here? She shook her head to clear the thoughts from her head. Why couldn't she enjoy a night out with her boy—

"If you don't want a burger, what about a salad?" Blue asked, cutting into her thoughts.

"I'm sorry," Raina said, smiling apologetically at him and the server. "An avocado burger with fries."

"You just said you didn't want a burger," Blue said. He gave her a strange look—a mix of confusion and anxiety.

The server was too well-trained to even blink.

"Yes, you're right." Raina flushed, sweat rolling down the small of her back. "A chicken Caesar salad. Thank you."

After the server left, Blue made several attempts at small talk. Raina tried to answer, but her eyes would stray to either Smith or Ralf and her voice would trail off. They sat in silence for several long minutes until the appetizer finally came out. She excused herself and rushed to the restroom.

Raina blotted her flushed face with a wet paper towel. This couldn't be happening. She didn't need this added stress of Smith and Ralf judging her girlfriend potential. She straightened, tucking an errant curl behind her ears. Focus. It was just a coincidence they were at the same restaurant. They were here to eat, just like she was.

By the time she got back to the table, her pep talk in the restroom had lost its power. She didn't understand what Smith and Ralf thought they could achieve by tailing her, but they weren't going to ruin her evening. She needed to relax and enjoy herself. Easy peasy.

Her heart pounded as she returned to her seat. A salad awaited her pleasure. Her throat was parched, and her hand, surprisingly, didn't shake when she reached for the glass of water.

"Everything okay?" Blue asked. His gold-flecked hazel eyes looked concerned.

"I'm fine," Raina whispered.

They chatted for the next few minutes, but she wouldn't be able to recall the subjects if her life depended on it. She should tell him the truth so he wouldn't think she wasn't interested. But what if the truth scared him away? This was her first real shot at a healthy relationship.

He nodded at the half-eaten salad. "The food is okay?"

"I'm on a diet," she said sheepishly, knowing he wouldn't believe her.

"I really like you, Sunshine, but tonight is worse than our first date."

She blinked at the tears welling up from behind her eyes. This was it. It isn't you. It's me. Goodbye and good luck. She'd heard it all before. "Are you breaking up with me?" She held her breath, afraid of the answer.

Blue opened his mouth, but the server returned with a dessert plate. He slid it onto the center of the table. "From the gentleman over there." He pointed to Smith, who gave them a curt wave.

Raina pasted a smile on her face and nodded her thanks.

"Who is that?" Blue asked. His face darkened with suspicion.

He had no idea how loaded the question was, but it wasn't in the direction his thoughts were heading. "He's the detective investigating Uncle Martin's death. What a coincidence to see him here," she said.

Blue's face cleared, and he didn't pursue the subject. "I thought you wanted to end things. You haven't been jumping with joy each time we've gotten together."

They had met last Christmas when she rushed out of a family party in tears, so it wasn't like he didn't know she had issues. But as Po Po would say, it was too early to show her granny panties.

"This isn't a good time for me. I'm still trying to wrap my head around Uncle Martin's death. I've known him my entire life. He was like another grandparent," she said. So it wasn't the full truth, but it was close enough.

"I'm sorry. Is there anything I can do to help?" he asked.

She glanced over Blue's shoulder to see both Smith and Ralf enjoying their dessert. She hoped they choked on it. "No, things will get better once I'm away from the city. I'm not my normal self here. It's like I'm wearing old clothes I've outgrown, so they are too tight on my skin. I'm not even sure I'm making any sense."

He reached for her hand. "I can see you're under pressure right now. We'll talk when you get home? In Gold Springs?"

When they parted half an hour later, Raina kissed him and told him how much she enjoyed being with him.

"Another place and another time," Blue said. "Got it."

Blue walked her back to her car and left. Raina felt like Scarlet O'Hara, watching Rhett walk away for the last time. She wasn't sure how much of it he got, but it was better than she'd expected. She'd sort it out when she wasn't so distracted with her family. After all, there was always tomorrow.

Raina drove back to Pacific Heights, circled the block once, and parked two blocks from the Victorian. The short walk in the dark wouldn't normally bother her, but her frayed nerves from her disastrous date with Blue made her jumpy. All she wanted to do was go home and soak in the tub. She tucked the ends of her scarf into her jacket and jammed her hands into her pockets. Hunching against the chill, she trotted toward the house.

The fog, gray-yellow under the streetlights, whirled around her, distorting her vision and muffling the regular traffic noise in a deceptive cocoon. Her heels clicked on the sidewalk and her breaths came out in a harsh whistle. She ignored the wet mist clinging to her face and hair.

Raina stopped ten feet away from the Victorian, squinting at the shadow in front of the gate. "Who's there?" she called out. Her hand tightened on her purse.

Silence.

Her heart pounded, and she told herself she was being silly. She took a step and stopped again.

The shape of a man separated from the shadows by the gate. As he stepped into the streetlight, the scar on the side of his mouth glowed silvery white. "We need to talk."

14

DEVIL'S BARGAIN

Raina took a step back and held her useless purse in front of her. "Take another step and I'll scream my head off." Like this would make any hardened criminal hesitate.

"Sweetheart, I might take you up on the offer at another time, but I'm cold from waiting for you to finish up your lame date. You can either come with me willingly or I can hogtie you. Your choice," Scar Face said.

She lowered her purse, heart pounding. She needed to get inside the house. "Where are we going?"

"How about the French place on Washington?" He looked her up and down. "You look like you need more food. The salad you ordered was a joke."

Fear settled like a concrete block on her chest. He was at the restaurant. When did she sign up to be Grand Marshal for the parade? "Hey! I eat plenty. I don't need someone like you feeding me and expecting things." Good, lighten up the mood.

Scar Face burst out laughing. "Fine, then invite me

up. I want to get out of this cold. A man can freeze his ba—"

"Who are you? And what do you want from me?"

As if knowing his name made things better. Her mom probably wasn't home, but Raina couldn't take the risk. What if her mom thought she was bringing home a new boyfriend? And Po Po was a wild card. Then there was her impressionable teenage brother. No, inviting him into the house was out of the question.

"Sonny Kwan. We need to talk about your grandfather's journal."

The new Dai Lo for the Nine Dragons? She glanced around but didn't see anything beyond their little bubble in the fog.

"I'm alone. You want to talk or what?"

Sonny Kwan was a beefy man, the kind who carried his weight like a weapon. Not only could he eat her for breakfast, but she barely had enough substance to fill the gaps between his teeth.

"I'm not sure being alone with you is good for my health," Raina said.

Sonny tucked his hands into his armpits. "Yeah, well, making me angry isn't good for your health."

No kidding, Raina thought. Was she willing to go into the house and close the door to what Sonny might have to say? And the man looked underdressed for the weather—a zipped-up nylon jacket over cuffed jeans that exposed his shins. "What happened to your clothes? Are you wearing cast-offs?"

Sonny shook his head. "I'm heading to the restaurant. Come if you want. Bring your posse. I'm leaving after one drink." He brushed past her and headed down the hill without looking to see if she would follow.

"Wait!" Raina called out before she was aware of her decision. She jogged after the triad leader. "I'm coming." She unwrapped her scarf and handed it to Sonny.

He seemed surprised and took it with a quick thanks.

The three-block trot was done in complete silence. The last thing she wanted was small talk. She yawned, wondering if her long day had clouded her judgment. Few people would be up for a walk in the fog with a triad boss. Someday her curiosity would get her in trouble.

Sonny held the door open for her when they got to the French restaurant. They found a table in the corner, and he planted himself so Raina couldn't see what happened behind her. It always made her antsy to fly blind like this. They ordered drinks and left the menus where the host placed them on the table.

He was like a wild hog in the candlelight, ready to barrel into the dressed-up people if he needed to. The cuffed pants now pulled up to his knees in his seated position, and the nylon jacket gave him tire rolls that normally weren't there. The other diners pointedly ignored the two of them, which meant they were very much aware of the disturbance in their refined world.

"I want your grandfather's journal. It contains information I want destroyed," Sonny said.

"I lost it when you shoved me in front of the train tracks," Raina snapped.

"It was an accident, and I apologized. I even sent back your purse, which was not even worth the courier fee."

Raina wondered if this kind of apology would work with her family. Getting insulted on her choice of clothing and accessories was getting old. "We both know that I don't have the journal. So why am I here?"

"You know that police officer? The guy who picked up the journal?"

"Detective Smith?"

"Yeah, him. He would do anything to get me behind bars. We'll trade me for the journal."

Raina gave Sonny a sideways glance. "What did you do to him? Kill his mother?" She sipped on her ice coffee. She was only half joking.

"Nah, nothing that serious." Sonny picked up his bottle of beer, pausing before he took a swallow. "We killed his fiancée."

She choked mid-swallow on the coffee, splattering it across the table and onto the triad boss's face.

Sonny jumped with an agility that surprised her. He blotted at his face with a crumpled napkin. "Hey! Watch it! I've killed people for less than this. If I knew you would be so uptight about his fiancée, I wouldn't have told you."

Raina grabbed a napkin, using the motion to hide her flash of fear. Idiot. She'd let the walk and atmosphere of the restaurant lull her into forgetting a career criminal sat across from her. "*We*, as in the Nine Dragons, or *we* as in *you*?"

He shrugged, returning to his seat. "Does it matter?"

"Actually, it does."

Sonny studied her for a fraction of a second. "Life is all about timing. When you walk in on a disagreement between rival gangs?" He shrugged. "So here's the plan. Tell Smith you want to trade a tip about a business deal for Monday night for your grandfather's journal. Tell him, Sonny Kwan might personally be there to oversee this shipment coming in through the Port of Oakland."

"I'm not sure your plan will work. First, how would I get this information? Second, why would Smith believe me and hand over police evidence?"

"I had someone check at the station, and the journal hasn't been logged. It's not in his apartment either, so he's carrying it around. I need to get it back."

She sat back, mulling over what he'd said. He could afford a rat in the police force, but he didn't want to send any of his goons to pick up the journal from Smith. It sounded like he also searched Smith's apartment.

"There's something in the journal you don't want your associates to know," she said. "What is it?"

"None of your business. Your job is to get me back the journal."

"What's in it for me? Why should I help you?"

"Your continued health."

She cocked her head, studying him. Why didn't he approach anyone else for help? "You don't want your associates to know Martin Eng almost ate your grandfather in China when he was a child."

The amusement left his eyes and his voice was grave. "I'll have to kill you now."

The blood drained from her face.

Sonny smiled, showing his back teeth like the big bad wolf. The scar on the side of his mouth moved with his smile like a silver worm under the skin. "I'm just kidding."

Her heart raced, and she had to tell herself to breathe. "Ha-ha. I'm laughing my as—"

"Another drink?" The waitress appeared, her small

round tray tucked into her armpits. She held a pen poised over her notebook. "How about an appetizer? Our chèvre truffles are to die for."

"The truffles sound good." Sonny glanced at Raina, his eyes twinkling. "You want anything else?"

Raina shook her head. The guy was toying with her. She had to think. Her grandfather saved his, which was the reason Ah Gong cashed in his chip with the Nine Dragons if she were to believe Po Po's stories. A life-debt was the only thing that made sense. And there was the package of firecrackers he'd left in her purse. If he didn't believe, then why would he want to ward off evil like an old Chinese farm wife?

She waited until the waitress left and held up seven fingers. "Seven generations. That's how long your family owes mine for saving your grandfather from the boiling pot." She forced a smile on her face, hoping it looked as predatory as his. "Don't worry, your secret is safe with me," she said, winking.

Her heart thudded. She felt like naked Barbie. Plastic perfect on the outside without an ounce of substance on the inside.

Sonny turned his head like a vulture over a carcass to study his competitor. He held up his beer in salute. "Touché."

The knot in her chest loosened, and she breathed again. "I can't let you destroy the journal before I read it. I'm trying to find out how my grandfather ended up with another family in China."

"You'll have plenty of time from when Smith delivers the journal to when I get out on bail."

Raina didn't want to argue with him. With his

contacts, he would be out within hours of his capture. "How did you even know the journal existed? I didn't even know of its existence until I went to my niece's birthday party."

"My grandfather told me about it years ago, but I haven't been able to track it down. Hudson Rice owes me protection money for his business. He called me when he saw you flashing around a leather book with the longevity symbol."

"I don't understand. Why didn't you get rid of the Rice family for this offense years ago?" She swallowed, but the question had to be asked. "Is this why you killed Martin Eng?"

"What kind of monster do you take me for?" He gave her a look as if he was tired of being misunderstood.

Oh, poor baby. She almost rolled her eyes, but it would have been a stupid move.

"Besides, we couldn't do anything while Martin was under your grandfather's protection," Sonny said.

She noticed he didn't answer her question about the murder. "So what happened to your clothes? You don't strike me as someone who shops at the Salvation Army store. I would think you're like Sonny Corinthos."

"Who?"

"Sonny. From *General Hospital*. The gangster."

"What kind of gang is *General Hospital*?"

"Never mind. It's a soap opera."

He looked at her as if she were nuts. And maybe she was for comparing him to the romanticized gangster on television. How could she not? They shared the same name.

"My organization is going through a restructure at the

moment," Sonny continued. "I wouldn't want a rumor like this to spread about its founding father. Cultural superstitions have no room in this modern age." He raised an eyebrow as if questioning her understanding of the situation.

Raina nodded at the implied threat. His recent ascent to the position of Dai Lo probably meant wolves were waiting to pull him down. He couldn't afford for his enemies to use this information to damage his credibility as a ruthless leader. When push came to shove, a life-debt could be conveniently forgotten. "Crystal clear. So how am I supposed to get Smith to believe me again?"

He handed her a note with the Nine Dragons chop stamped on it. "Use your imagination."

FUNNY MONEY

Raina woke the next morning to burning bacon and loud banging doors. Without even heading downstairs, she knew her mom made breakfast. She glanced at the display on her cell phone. Six thirty in the morning. Something was up because her mom wasn't a morning person.

She rolled out of bed and headed toward the guest bathroom. As much as she wanted to sleep, there wouldn't be any rest when Mom got a burr in her saddle. When she got out of the shower, someone pounded on the door.

"Breakfast, honey," Mom called out.

"Okay," Raina said.

"Breakfast!"

"Okay," Raina yelled.

"Just making sure you heard me."

"Okay."

Fifteen minutes later, Raina sat next to a snoring Po Po at the dining room table. Mom and Hudson bustled back and forth from the kitchen with plates of food. When the couple returned to the kitchen for cups of coffee and tea, she poked her grandma until she woke up.

"Why aren't we in bed?" Po Po yawned, showing the amalgam fillings in her molars.

"You tell me. Why are they making us breakfast?" Raina whispered. "It's not even eight yet."

"I wish they got a big breakfast from Mikey D's instead. I can't believe I have to pretend to eat this stuff again. Apparently, cooking skills don't get better with age. The last time your mom made me a meal was when she was sixteen and she passed her driving test." Her grandma spooned runny eggs onto a plate. "She wanted a car then."

Mom came in from the kitchen, holding out two steaming cups. "Tea and coffee for my two favorite girls." She set the cups in front of them.

Raina thanked her mom and stabbed a piece of burnt bacon. What was her mom up to? Plaster would have to stand aside for the layer her mom was slathering on.

Hudson came back into the room and handed Mom a cup of coffee. "How's the food?" He glanced from Po Po to Raina, his smile eager.

"Great," Raina mumbled around the bacon in her mouth.

"Wonderful," Po Po said, sipping the tea.

"Have some more." He splattered a large heaping of eggs on Raina's plate. "Eat up."

Raina pointed at her grandma. "Don't forget Po Po."

Her grandma shot her a look. "This grub is just great." She shoved a spoonful of slimy eggs under a piece of cardboard toast. "To what do we owe this fabulous meal?"

Mom glanced at Hudson and then smiled at Raina. "I told Hudson about your little plan to investigate Uncle Martin's death. We want to help."

Great. The two of them wanted to play detective. What was next? A tea party? "You're doing a great job now, Mom," Raina said. "If I need any help, I'll let you know."

"He's my uncle. I need to help. I feel so useless just waiting around," Hudson said.

"How about you take care of your sister first?" Raina said. "She's trying to clean up and leave her abusive boyfriend."

"Raina!" Mom sounded shocked. "There's no need—"

Hudson held up a hand. "I deserve this. It's hard to help someone who thinks you're the enemy. She shouldn't have hooked up with the wrong man. I can understand why Uncle Martin didn't want to rely on someone so unpredictable at his age."

"Family doesn't give up on each other," Raina said, glancing at her mom. If they did, she would have found herself another parent by now. "Besides I've hit a brick wall. The suspects either have alibis or no motives." And she wasn't ready to share Sonny's plan with her mom and her boyfriend.

"What about the business rival?" Mom asked.

"She seems prosperous. I don't think her argument with Martin harmed her at all," Po Po said. "She has no motive to harm him."

"Are you sure? Some people look like they are doing well on the outside, but are secretly broke," Hudson said.

"You can always ask her yourself. She'll be over later

this morning to do something about Weeping May," Po Po said.

Hudson blinked but was too polite to ask about the ghost haunting their house.

Mom was under no compunction. "How come you didn't hire Hudson to take care of it? A stranger will not be as invested as family to remove this presence. He's practically family."

"It's okay, honey." Hudson patted mom's hand. "We shouldn't encourage nepotism."

"Our family defined nepotism." Mom stood. "I guess we know where we stand in this family. Come on, Hudson, we have stuff to do." She sailed out of the dining room. Hudson gave Raina and Po Po an apologetic look and followed her.

The hall closet opened and closed. There was the clatter of putting on shoes, the swish of gathering jackets and scarves, and finally the click of the front door closing.

As the silence seeped through the house, Raina released the breath she'd been holding.

"I thought they would never leave," Po Po said. "This sounds horrible, and you know I love your mother, but sometimes it's hard to be around her."

"I thought mothers are supposed to always want to spend time with their children," Raina said.

"Not always."

Raina pressed her lips into a thin line. Was there something wrong with her personality? She couldn't seem to get along with either her mom or her sister.

Po Po squeezed her hands as if she'd read her mind. "It's not you. It's them."

She smiled, feeling better. "This is what my ex-boyfriends always say right before they break up with me."

"Speaking of date, how did it go last night? You came home late." Her grandma wiggled her eyebrows. "Did you guys get hot and heavy?"

"Po Po!"

"Oh, come on. We're both adults. It's not like I get to have a hot and heavy date. My dates are a success when their dentures stay in place during the goodnight kiss."

Raina covered her ears with her hands. "La-la-la. I don't need to hear this stuff. Please save it for your BFF." What could she do to erase the vision of her grandma getting hot and heavy in a make-out session? Did Po Po say these things to shock her or did she really do them? "Sonny Kwan was waiting for me when I got home."

Po Po rubbed her hands together. "This is going to be juicy. I can feel it in my bones. Give me all the details."

"Aren't you worried about my safety? I got abducted by a triad boss."

Her grandma's gaze traveled the length of her. "You seem fine. I have no doubts you can take him on."

"Thanks for the vote of confidence even though I don't agree with you." She told her grandma Sonny's plan for getting the journal back from the police. "How much can I trust a person like Sonny? I need to take this chance; otherwise, I have nothing to bargain with Smith."

"I don't like this."

"Even if Smith says no, I'd be perfectly safe. The SFPD wouldn't harm me."

"It's not him I'm worried about—it's Sonny. When does he plan to get the journal back from you? He has killed before; how do we know he wouldn't do it again? An old family debt is the only thing protecting you."

"I don't have any choice." Raina gave her grandma a sideways glance. "Unless we stop searching for Ah Gong's secret family? There's no one alive who could tell us what happened."

Po Po averted her gaze. She probably came to the same conclusion. "There's Sonny's grandfather."

"And you think it would be any less dangerous to find a retired Dai Lo hiding from his enemies?" Raina shook her head. "No, I have to partner with Sonny."

RAINA HELPED CARRY the uneaten food back into the kitchen. Her eyes widened at the unwashed pots and pans in the double sink. Dribbles of congealing eggs and bacon grease decorated the island and countertops. "It looks as if they used every pan in the house."

Po Po sighed, rolling up her sleeves. "It's the gift that keeps on giving."

"I can take care of this," Raina said.

"No, no. We need you to contact Smith. Joley Mok will be here in an hour, and I don't want her to see this mess."

Win came in, took one look at the sink, and said, "I'm having a Pop-tart." While the pastry warmed in the toaster, he wiped the island. "We should ban Mom from the kitchen."

"How was the drive to Napa? No problems with Brandi checking in at the rehab center?" Po Po asked.

"It was fine." He grabbed his breakfast and left for the

matinee with his girlfriend. So much for a morning conversation.

Raina strolled out to the living room, dialing Smith's cell phone number. As the phone rang, she peered out the window and didn't see any car sitting outside watching the house.

Both Sonny and Smith had put the ball in her court. At this point, there was no reason to watch what she did. And boy, did she want to play...except she had no idea if she was even in the right court.

After several rings, she got Smith's voicemail. She left him a brief message she wanted to meet later in the after-noon to discuss his earlier proposition to team up on the investigation. As she hung up, a Mini Cooper parked half a block away. A large man stepped out, unfurling until he reached his full height beside the clown car. She watched Joley and Ralf grab the tools of their trade and head toward the house.

It triggered a stray comment from her conversation with Mrs. Keane. She had mentioned a woman leaving Martin's townhouse in a Mini Cooper right before his death. Was it possible that Joley Mok visited Martin the night of his murder?

Raina greeted them and sent them on to the kitchen. She would let them work their magic on Weeping May, and then when they were relaxed, spring the question on them to gauge their reactions. Easy peasy.

"Wong Po Po, can you tell us more about Weeping May?" Joley asked.

"There's not much to say. She threw herself off the balcony in the 1920s when she was jilted at the altar. After that, the house went through several owners, each of them owning the place for a year or two. That's how we got this house at a bargain price in the mid-sixties."

"I don't feel any disturbance here." Joley pulled out the Chinese compass and watched the whirling magnetic needle. "But something is not quite right. Let's go upstairs."

"What were you doing at Uncle Martin's house after eleven o'clock the evening before his death?" Raina asked, cutting in before the three of them headed upstairs. Forget the plan. Might as well get the confrontation over with.

"I don't know what you're talking about," Joley said. Ralf glanced at her, but she ignored him.

"An eyewitness places you at the scene of the crime. Tall, thin, Chinese woman driving a Mini Cooper," Raina said.

"Could be an unreliable witness. I was nowhere near the Richmond District."

Po Po's head swiveled between Raina and Joley during the entire conversation like a Ping-Pong ball bouncing across the net. "Who is your source?"

Raina shrugged. "This person would have told the police about Joley's appearance at the townhouse by now." She gave the feng shui master a pointed look. "Don't say I didn't warn you, but you can expect a visit from the police sometime soon."

Ralf glanced at Joley. "We have nothing to hide."

"Then why were you watching me at the restaurant?" Raina asked.

Ralf glanced at Po Po. "Ah..."

"I hired him to keep an eye on you," her grandma

said. "With the Nine Dragons popping up, I thought it was a good idea."

Fine job he did, Raina thought. She returned her attention to the PI. "Well?"

Joley glanced at Ralf, narrowing her eyes. "Fine. I was there, but it was not what you think. I don't like talking about my client's business with other people."

Raina's eyes widened. Martin wouldn't have hired Joley for feng shui because he could take care of it himself. "To do some PI work? Who did he ask you to tail?"

Joley studied her. "You're too sharp to be wasting your time as a history grad student. Martin was worried about the family business. I've been keeping tabs on Hudson for him. Once a week, I came by to give him an update. It was usually late in the evening so there was little chance I would run into his nephew."

"What do you mean by keeping tabs on Hudson?"

"Exactly that. Following people as they go about their business is part of my business."

"What did you found out?"

"It was just as Martin suspected. Business is in the toilet because there aren't that many Chinese families who would trust someone who is half Chinese. It didn't help that Hudson lived in LA for the last twenty years when he could have used the time to become part of the community."

"Isn't that discrimination?" Po Po asked.

"When you're in the business of dealing with faith and superstition, everything counts. Race, lucky underwear—doesn't matter. Martin Eng was good enough because he had been in Chinatown for the last forty years. When he retired, his regulars didn't trust his nephew." Joley hesitated, glancing at Ralf. "Many of them became my clients, but I didn't have to solicit their business."

"Does Hudson have any money?" Raina asked. She hated sounding like Cassie, but if he had no money of his own then he might want an older wealthy woman to take care of him...like her mom.

Except, no one outside the family knew that she was broke, having gone through her trust fund before she was forty. Without Po Po's generosity, Mom wouldn't be able to prance around town like she was still a socialite. If not for the money Ah Gong had already set aside for her brother, Raina had no idea how they would pay for his college education.

"What are you trying to say, Rainy? That Hudson killed Martin for his money?" Po Po shook her head. "The idea is just outrageous."

"This question had to be asked. Just because he's my mom's boyfriend doesn't automatically rule him out," Raina said. Although she couldn't see how he could physically murder Martin when he was with her mother the entire evening. She shook the image of the two of them making out at the dining room table in the wee hours of the morning from her mind.

Po Po glared at Raina. "I don't like where these questions are headed. The boy grew up around my children like he was one of my own. If he had a tendency for violence, I would have known it."

"Do you have any proof?" Raina blabbered, knowing full well her grandma would think she was being rude to her guest.

"Rain—"

Joley held out her cell phone. "It's okay, Wong Po Po. Here are the emails we've been trading back and forth."

Raina didn't even glance at the display. If the ghost whisperer wasn't lying, then her mom's future fiancé was as broke as she was. Good grief.

"Martin was afraid his nephew would run the family business to the ground—which is a matter of time. Why do you think Hudson has so much free time to spend with your mom, Raina?" Joley asked.

Good question, but one Raina didn't have an answer to. Now it looked like she had to add busting up her mom's relationship on her to-do list.

Her cell phone dinged, indicating a new text message. She pulled it out from her pocket. It was from Smith and he wanted to meet in two hours.

16

NINJA ATTACK

Joley and Ralf left after doing their magic upstairs, promising to come back if Po Po still felt Weeping May's presence. While Raina put little stock in the "exorcism," the guest bathroom was less drafty.

Growing up with her entire community worshiping ancestors and various deities depending on the situation, she had a healthy respect for the supernatural. If nothing else, it never hurt to tread lightly on other people's beliefs.

Raina wanted to ask for advice on how to handle the situation with Hudson and her mom, but Po Po avoided the topic by fiddling with her cell phone. While her grandma was gung-ho on every other aspect of her life, she preferred avoidance when it came to familial discord.

They returned to the kitchen to scavenge for lunch. The last person to go grocery shopping was Raina earlier in the week. She sighed at the bare shelves and the limp lettuce.

"Smith wants to meet at the Japanese Tea Garden in Golden Gate Park," Raina said, pulling deli lunch meat from the refrigerator. Maybe they should go out for food.

"Why there?" Po Po asked.

"No idea. Maybe he's on duty and it would be less likely for someone to see him inside a paid venue."

Po Po handed her a keychain with a ball on a string. "Attach it to your keys, Rainy. It might come in handy someday."

"Is this a good luck charm?"

"No, it's a weapon of mass destruction."

Raina eyed the keychain but attached it to her keys as directed. Granted the string was a heavy corded lanyard and the wrapped ball appeared to have weight to it, but a weapon of mass destruction?

"Allow me to demonstrate," Po Po said, pulling her keys from her pocket. "Give me yours so you can see the two of them working in tandem."

Raina handed over her keys and took a step back.

Po Po got into a self-defense stance, arms up with keys in each hand, the ball keychain dangling at the end. "Now stand back. I don't want to knock you out by mistake."

Her grandma took a deep breath. "En garde, you rogue." She swept her arms from side to side, the balls flying at an alarming angle. She inched forward like she was fencing.

"Careful," Raina called out, afraid the balls would ricochet against the wall and hit her grandma in the face.

Now Po Po really got into her act, alternating between jabs and punches. The balls bounced in the air like toy nunchucks.

A ball slammed into the lucky cat clock, smashing in the plastic display. It slid off the wall and crashed onto the tile floor, scattering plastic pieces all over the kitchen. Her grandma tried to stop, but the momentum of her other arm knocked a hole in the drywall where the clock once hung. The silence after the crash could have done a librarian proud.

"Well, I never liked the clock," Po Po said. "It was from Ah Gong after we got into an argument about tie clips."

Raina gave her grandma a sideways glance. "So what is this weapon of mass destruction called?"

"Monkey Ball," Po Po announced proudly. "It's to keep my dates from getting too frisky."

Raina plugged her fingers into her ears. "La-la-la." She didn't want to hear about her seventy-five-year-old grandma getting frisky. "Let's roll. We can grab lunch on the way to the meeting spot."

As she drove, Raina wondered if she'd embraced the idea of Hudson being a charlatan because she secretly didn't want her mother's relationship to work out. As the only girl and baby of the family, her mom could be a tad selfish at times. While Raina's dad was alive, she kept that side of her under control because of his expectation for a partner in the marriage.

After his death, when she moved the family back to her childhood home, she'd relied on the grandparents to be the parents to the Sun children. And after a decade of book and wine clubs, shopping, and charity events, she'd finally fallen in love again.

If Raina found evidence of Hudson's financial ineptitude, she would burst this little bubble of happiness. Or maybe it was love, and the lack of money from either party wasn't an issue. And dan tats could fly.

It was obvious her grandma wanted nothing to do with this drama. A worm on a sidewalk after a rainstorm was more comfortable than the position Raina was in.

They ate in the car and got to the tea garden ten minutes early. For a weekend, the place wasn't crowded. They could talk to each other without feeling like they had to speak over the person behind them. They had Drum Bridge to themselves for the moment. The high arch wood bridge belonged to a Japanese village in the early 1900s.

Po Po pointed to a bonsai tree next to the five-story pagoda across the pond. "I will be there. Don't worry, I'll be watching you the whole time."

"Okay," Raina said, dragging the word out. "Or you can just stay here."

"No, I don't want Smith to notice me. He might ask me questions. Besides, I can use my binoculars and block my face with a magazine over there." Po Po strolled off. "Ta-ta," she called over her shoulder.

Raina snorted in amusement. Yes, hiding behind a magazine with a backpack the size of a small country in purple camo was definitely less noticeable. And where was her grandma buying these camo outfits?

She squinted against the glare bouncing off the water and peeled off her jacket. It felt like a spring day rather than the middle of winter. The koi fishes flashed around the pond, rushing to every shadow with opened mouths.

Footsteps thudded against the floor planks and she turned to see Smith at the foot of the bridge. He could be considered handsome, but he had the demeanor of a tiny man who needed to strut like a puffed rooster. His polo shirt and jeans were tight as ever and his blonde hair just as big.

"I'm glad you gave my proposition some thought," Smith said. "I can give you an endorsement for your private investigator license." Since she stood at the top of the arch, he met her eye to eye.

"I have no plans on becoming a PI," Raina said. And when did a cop's endorsement matter?

"Isn't this why you called me? So you can tag along on the investigation for Martin Eng's murder?"

"No. I want my grandfather's journal, and I know you have it. I'm here to trade information for it."

Smith studied her like she was a bimbolina. If Raina cared, she would be insulted. As it was, she found it amusing he would dismiss her. "I'm not sure your information is of any value to me."

"How about the date and time of the shipment to bring in your fiancée's murderer—Sonny Kwan."

Smith's expression didn't change, but the vein on the side of his neck throbbed. "Ah, I see. Aiding and abetting a known felon could get you thrown in prison. Tell me everything you know about the Nine Dragons, and I could get you off on probation."

If Raina's eyebrows could go any higher, they would touch her hairline. Was he trying to scare her into becoming a police informant? "What are you talking about?"

"Your grandfather had ties to the triad. The arrangement is probably passed to someone in your family. I'm surprised this person is you. Tell me what you know, and

I can help you. Getting involved with hardened criminals can ruin your life."

Raina turned away from him, glancing down at the pond. A silver and black koi fish about the size of a log whipped water against a rock and headed toward the food tossed into the opposite bank. She didn't even know how to answer Smith.

Pretending to be part of the organization would be idiotic. She didn't need to be on the police radar any more than she already was. But how could she get Smith to believe her information would help him capture Sonny without being a triad snitch?

"You might have grabbed the journal, but I picked up a note." She glanced up at him. "A man with a scar next to his mouth pushed me onto the rail at the BART station a few nights ago. It was crowded, and I stood too close to the edge. After describing the scar to the Chinese community, I found out he is Sonny Kwan, Dai Lo of the Nine Dragons." She shuddered, which was real enough. "If I'd known who he was before, I would have run the opposite direction rather than chase him."

Smith sighed as if she missed her boat. "A tiny little girl like you isn't going to last long locked up with the hardened criminals. Call me when you change your mind and want to be a police informant."

He left without a backward glance. If he thought she was connected to the triad, then her information could misdirect the police from an actual operation. His offer to take her on as a police informant was ludicrous, except now she was back to square one.

Sonny's plan was a long shot, but she secretly hoped it might recover her grandfather's journal. At least now she could return her focus to investigating Martin's murder and looking into Hudson's finances.

She trotted to the bonsai tree, but didn't see any purple camo. Where did her grandma go? She pulled out her cell phone, but before she could dial Po Po's number, she heard shuffling in the shrubs behind her.

Whack! Thump!

Alarmed, she backed away and slowly circled the shrubs while the whacking and thumping continued.

"Stop! I'm not a hit man!" a man called out.

Hudson?

Raina peered through the vegetation and saw Po Po on the back of a man, her short legs wrapped around his thick waist, one arm curled under his throat, and her other hand whacking him with the Monkey Fist. The overhanging vegetation prevented her grandma from maneuvering the weapon of mass destruction with any momentum or she would have done real damage to her future son-in-law. As it was, she was like a buzzing fly that one would swat under a different circumstance.

When the man turned, Raina wanted to laugh at Hudson's clenched teeth and raised arms, trying to ward off her grandmother without harming her. If he hadn't second-guessed his desire to be part of the family, now would be a good time.

"It's Hudson! Po Po, stop," Raina yelled.

Po Po slid off his back, wheezing, and bent over her knees. "Geez, I could have split your head like a watermelon. What are you doing skulking about in the bushes?"

"I was trying to do my part in the investigation. Your

mother was right—it's a carnival around you two. Why would a hitman be after you?"

"What do you expect? I was incognito and yet you still managed to sneak up on me."

"Purple camo, pimp cane, a small backpack with a canteen. You blended with the environment. Must be my X-ray vision."

Po Po glowered at him and addressed Raina. "How did it go? Did Smith want to trade?"

She shook her head, both to her grandma's antics and to answer her question. "Smith thinks I am part of the Nine Dragons. He offered me the job of being the snitch."

"You can't do that. The triad would hunt you down," Hudson said, his voice full of concern. "When did you become involved with the triad? Does your mother know?"

She eyed her future stepfather. "I don't understand how Smith got the impression I'm even remotely connected to the triad. It's good you're here, Hudson. There's something I've wanted to ask you. Did you call Sonny Kwan about my grandfather's journal?"

Hudson's eyes widened, his thoughts racing across his face—from chagrin to guilt. "Yes, but I didn't expect you to get hurt. If Win hadn't said something, we'd never know. I can't believe you kept being pushed onto the train tracks a secret."

"Oh, just stop it," Po Po said. "You're not her father. There's no need to get on this high horse."

Hudson flushed in embarrassment. "You don't know what it's like to have the triad breathing down your neck for protection money. Being a small business owner isn't fun and games—"

Raina held up her hand to stop his babbling. "Why are you with my mother?"

"Because I love her."

"What if I tell you she has no money left in her trust fund? That she is living on the charity of her family?"

He sneaked a glance at Po Po. "I don't see how this is relevant. It's not like we're getting married."

"Now wait just a minute," Po Po cut in. "Are you trifling with her feelings? Are you telling me, young man, you have no intentions of proposing to my daughter?"

Hudson grew even redder, the flush deepening to his throat. "The two of us have an understanding. At our age, we want companionship, but no strings. We're both on the same page about marriage." He folded his hands over his potbelly as if to end the discussion on his love life.

Oh no. Her mom would get her heart broken by this man. Raina curled her hands and tucked them into her armpits. He was lucky they were out in public, or she might grab her grandma's keychain and give him a whack or two herself. Now how was she to convey his message to her mother without getting shot? It was much easier to be the worm on the sidewalk than a messenger bearing bad news.

17

KILL THE MESSENGER

Raina spent the rest of the day dragging out boxes from the attic. She made three trips to donate vintage clothing, eight-track tapes, and several tubs of Christmas stuff. How did one person collect ten Christmas trees? It wasn't like her grandma put up more than one at a time.

By the time evening rolled around, she was beat. She took a quick shower, threw on some clothes, and drove to her Uncle Sain's restaurant for the Chinese New Year's Eve family dinner. With a family the size of theirs—sixty members just from Ah Gong and Po Po's branch alone and another rotating dozen of second cousins and family friends—the Wongs were lucky to have access to a banquet room normally reserved for weddings and birthday parties.

When Raina stepped into the restaurant, she felt the electric buzz of family gossip fill the air. Her cousin, Jung-yee, flittered from grouping to grouping like a hummingbird, dipping into every conversation long enough to impart her news. Mom beamed at the ongoings and surrounded by her sisters-in-law. Hudson was in a similar group filled with her uncles.

Po Po had decorated the restaurant with her daughters-in-law all day. Red tablecloths, gleaming glassware, and bouquets of flowers on the round tables. The music was festive, playing the traditional Cantonese songs for the holiday. The uncles' pockets and aunts' purses bulged with red envelopes filled with five-dollar bills. They passed the envelopes out to the children, who wished them a prosperous new year. The room looked good, but her grandma would have a fit if she knew the place screamed of an engagement party.

Raina's heart sank as her mind processed the situation. She couldn't believe Hudson proposed after he said he wasn't ready for a commitment. The liar. And apparently the news her mom was broke didn't matter. Could this be love? Or the thought of Po Po's purse strings widening to welcome him into the family?

She grabbed her sister Cassie's arm and dragged her away from discussion on dress styles for a spring wedding. "We need to talk. It's about Mom."

"Oh, did she tell you already? I'm so happy for her," Cassie said. She held out a red envelope. "What you do say, little sister?"

Since Raina wasn't married, traditionally she was still considered a child even though she was in her late twenties. "Gong Hey Fat Choy." She rushed through the happy new year blessing and pocketed the envelope. "Hudson is broke. He either believes Mom still has money in her trust fund or Po Po would support the two of them," she whispered, feeling like dirt for raining on everyone's parade. Why couldn't she just be happy for the couple?

The smile slipped from Cassie's face. "But he inherited the family business from Uncle Martin—"

"Which he ran to the ground. How many Chinese families do you know use his services?"

"Sh—"

"We need to do something. If he's looking for a sugar mama, Mom is the wrong person. Imagine waking up one morning to Mom, Hudson, and Win at your doorstep." She pinched her index finger and thumb together. "Po Po is already this close to kicking Mom out on her butt. You really think she'll welcome a bum for a son-in-law?"

"What do we do?"

"Have they announced their engagement yet?"

"No, but Jung-yee is making great strides to letting everyone in on the secret. I think they are planning to announce it before the Longevity Noodles come out from the kitchen."

Every dish for the Chinese New Year's Eve dinner was symbolic of well wishes for the upcoming year. Longevity Noodles were extra-long noodles meant to represent a long life.

"I guess we'll just have to bust up their plans before then," Raina said.

"My gosh, this is such horrible timing. She'll never forgive us. To have a broken heart for the rest of the year..." Her sister shuddered at the idea.

"Would you rather they announce their engagement,

be congratulated by all our family and friends over the next few days, and then break up after the Chinese New Year celebrations?"

Cassie grimaced. "That would be even worse. Okay, so when are you going to tell her? I'll keep everyone out of your way. I'll even have Lila create a distraction if it helps."

"Me? Why do I have to tell her? Why not you? You're her favorite."

"You're the one with the firsthand information. What I have to say is hearsay. You should do it."

Raina grabbed a flute of champagne from the passing waitress. She downed it in one gulp. "This will only make her hate me more." Her relationship with her mom was tenuous enough as it was, but this would be the final blow. Her mom might never speak to her again after this.

"Mom doesn't hate you. Stop being so dramatic." Cassie smiled and exchanged words with a passing cousin, pretending like they were discussing the weather for all the emotion she showed on her face.

Easy for her sister to say. She was the golden child who could do no wrong in their mother's eyes. And to top it off, she was married with a grandchild, while Raina was still treading water as far as their mother was concerned.

The cousin left, and Cassie re-focused on Raina. "Uncle Anthony is calling for us to take our seats. You better grab Mom before dinner starts." And with that, she returned to her husband's side. What moral support.

Raina had meant to drag Mom away from the crowd but somehow ended up sitting across from her and Hudson at the large round table. There was no way she could have a word without either shouting across the table or getting out from her chair. Now what?

With Jung-yee at the table with her new boyfriend, Po Po and her cousin, Win and his girlfriend, Raina was the only unpaired person. The empty spot next to her shouted her singleness. Why did she even show up?

"What happened to your boyfriend?" Jung-yee asked, her voice dripping with sweetness. "Is he running late?"

Raina held out her wineglass to Hudson, who was busy making sure everyone had alcohol for a toast. "He can't make it tonight." She hadn't invited Blue, but the family didn't need to know this.

Jung-yee smirked. "Oh, that's too bad. What about Matthew? He rarely misses our family dinners."

Raina downed half the Chardonnay in one gulp. "He's taking care of his grandma." Her ex-boyfriend and his grandma were pseudo members of the Wong's extensive family. Not only had Raina grown up with him and later dated him, but she also saw him at various family functions throughout the year. Her life was a series of awkward situations that amused everyone else but her.

Hudson leaned down, whispering something in Mom's ear, causing her to giggle and casting her eyes away from him in mock bashfulness. Raina caught her eye, and Mom raised her glass.

She did the same and downed the rest of her wine, reaching for a refill. Win moved the bottle and handed her a can of 7-Up instead. Party pooper. He frowned but returned to his conversation with his girlfriend.

The alcohol was already doing its magic. The Chinese music blaring from the hidden speakers jangled and pealed, setting an upbeat mood for the room. The stomach churning turned into hunger, and she salivated, watching the plates of food sail out from the kitchen.

Plates of noodles for longevity. Steamed catfish in soy sauce for surpluses or savings. Dumplings shaped like ancient silver ingots for wealth. Golden brown egg rolls for bars of gold. Every dish required a cryptologist to decipher its secret meaning for the hidden blessing of wealth, good fortune, and health. The Chinese community was a superstitious lot all right.

Raina soon lost track of the dishes coming from the kitchen. She ended up with an emptied beer bottle in front of her, and when she glanced at her brother suspiciously, he was the one to wag a finger like she should stop drinking.

With a full belly, a slight buzz that blurred the talons among her family, and no engagement announcement, the tension on her shoulders melted. Her head became heavy, and she floated above the conversation.

Tink. tink. tink.

Raina jerked awake and glanced around. Hudson towered in front of her, banging his chopstick on the glass in his hand like a gong. The conversation eventually died down.

She glanced at all the beaming smiles, and Cassie gave her a look as if to say "do something." Po Po was nowhere in sight. Probably hiding out in the restroom so she wouldn't have to say anything. Her grandma only liked public confrontation when the subject didn't matter, and she wanted to be a contrarian.

Hudson cleared his throat, pulling at the collar of his shirt. Her mom gazed up at him, the picture perfect blushing bride-to-be. They were a handsome couple. Distinguished and carefree since neither worked a day in their lives. Some people even might say they were well suited.

Raina choked on the last of her wine. Glasses were being refilled as Hudson held his glass in front of him to prepare for a toast. Geez, why did she always have to be the bad guy? She stood, swaying and held up her empty wineglass. "I have something to get off my chest. Ya'll could be my intervention." Her words slurred a little, but it rang loud and clear across the room. If the room wasn't quiet before, she could hear a pin drop now.

Hudson blinked as the attention shifted away from him. "Um..." He glanced at Mom. "Are you sure it can't wait?"

Win tugged at her arm. "Sis, you should sit down."

Her mother's eyes were huge, a hint of fear shone from behind the trembling smile.

Raina jerked her arm away from her brother. The time to sit it out was long gone. "Ah Gong left me the three million dollars so I could send it to his secret family in China." She continued with the details of how she came to be the secret keeper in the weeks leading up to his death. By the middle of her tale, Hudson slid back into his chair, probably guessing now wasn't the appropriate time for his announcement.

She glanced around at the familiar faces. They were a sea of confusion, anger, and disbelief. She almost laughed at the open gaping on her cousin Jung-yee's face. Her brother-in-law, Benson, had a calculating look, as if he wondered how to profit from this news.

By the time she finished, the only sound that could be

heard was the noise coming from the kitchen. Even the wait staff held their breaths by the entryway into the banquet room, afraid to interrupt the family powwow with more food and drink.

"I'm sorry I've kept everyone in the dark for so long, but I want to start the Year of the Monkey off right. Thank you and good-night," Raina said, saluting for some stupid reason.

As she lowered herself into the chair, her glance strayed to the threshold leading to the restrooms. Po Po stood frozen, a horrified expression on her face. A flash of heat raced up Raina's neck and the air went out of her lungs, and she crashed into her chair. It tipped, spilling her onto the floor. She laid still, struggling to breathe. By saving her mother, she had destroyed her grandma instead.

THE NEXT MORNING, Raina nursed a steaming cup of plain black coffee by herself at the kitchen island. The rain outside pounded against the house in time with her throbbing head. Her eyes were swollen from crying herself to sleep. She wished she were home so she could commiserate with her BFFs—Ben and Jerry. A little Cherry Garcia would go a long way to helping her welcome the Year of the Monkey.

She could blame it on the alcohol, but it would be a lie. The desire to let the secret out had been threatening to spill for weeks now. She'd tried to convince her grandma it needed to come out, but it fell on deaf ears. Did she do it to thumb her nose at Po Po?

Win strolled into the kitchen, took one look at her, and said, "Where's breakfast? I'm starting to have expectations with you home and in the kitchen."

Raina shot daggers at him. "You're funny, baby brother."

Win got a box of eggs out of the refrigerator. "Aw, come on. Make me something. You always feel better after fiddling around in the kitchen. And punishing yourself with plain black coffee is just stupid." He popped a hazelnut k-cup into the brewer.

As the aromatic scent filled the kitchen, Raina admitted her teenage brother was more perceptive than she gave him credit for. "Thanks for the ride home last night. Sorry, I cut your evening short with your girlfriend."

He slid the hazelnut coffee in front of her. "Not a problem, as long as you feed me."

She took a sip, inhaling deeply. "Fine. Get me the cutting board."

For the next few minutes, they worked in the kitchen companionably. Her brother was the perfect helper, doing the wash-up in between runs to the refrigerator. The egg sausage muffin pizzas came out of the oven piping hot with a light crunch. Each bite made her feel better.

"So what's wrong with Hudson?" Win asked, rubbing his stomach and pushing the plate aside.

"I don't know what you're talking about."

"You've kept Ah Gong's secret for years, what's another day? And yet, you chose the moment when Hudson wanted to announce his engagement. There's no way he can top a bomb like that. So why don't you want him to be our stepfather?"

"Are you sure you're only seventeen?"

"What can I say? I'm mature for my years."

She told him about her conversation with Joley Mok. "Hudson said he wasn't interested in marriage when I asked him about it at the Japanese Tea Garden. I wonder what changed his mind. He knows Mom has no money of her own."

"Maybe it's really love."

Raina gave him a sideways glance. He was still young enough to never have a broken heart. She didn't want to burst his bubble—their family was cursed in the relationship department. Look at their grandma, Mom, and older sister. "You could be right."

"Or you can ask Brandi? She'd give you the dirt on her brother. They take sibling rivalry to a whole new level."

"I might just do that."

"What are you going to do about Po Po?"

A lump formed in Raina's throat. She blinked rapidly at the tears behind her eyes. "I don't know," she whispered. "This is the second time we fought about how I dealt with Ah Gong's secret. She begged me not to say anything..."

He patted her hand. "I wouldn't choose such a setting, but Chinese New Year is the time to clear old debts and skeletons."

As she clutched his hand like it was a lifeline, a tear rolled down her face. She had done nothing to cause her ancestors to punish her by taking away her relationship with her beloved grandma.

No, she needed to have faith everything would work out. There was a lesson here, and she had to learn it to break this cycle in her life...now if only she knew what this lesson was.

18

DANCING FOOL

Raina dug in her purse for her cell phone. Her fingers brushed the pack of firecrackers and she held it up. "We should light this after dinner tonight. You better move it if you want to get to school on time. I can clean up the kitchen after I talk to Brandi."

She called the rehab center, listened to the selections on the automated service, and prayed punching zeros would get her connected to a live person. The phone rang and she got a receptionist. "I would like to speak to Brandi Rice, please."

"Sure, hon," said the cheerful voice.

There was a click and then the phone rang. Several more rings and she got disconnected. She dialed the main line again, going through the same song and dance with the automated service. When she got the receptionist again, she asked, "Could you check on Brandi Rice to make sure she's okay?"

"I'm the only one at the reception desk right now. I'll

call the nurse's station to see if someone is available. She will call you back within an hour," said the friendly voice in the phone line.

"An hour?"

"The patients should be in their morning counseling session right now. If Brandi isn't in her room, then she's in a session. We wouldn't want to interrupt her treatment plan, would we?"

"No, of course not. Please call me back."

Raina left them her cell phone number with little hope she would get a return call. She glanced at the hole next to where the lucky cat once hung on the drywall. She should get someone to get the wall repaired. She called her best friends instead.

Eden picked up on the second ring. "Hey, girl, how are you doing?"

She cradled the phone with her shoulder, taking all the red envelopes out of her purse. "Counting all the red envelopes I got last night."

"I wish I could have made it to dinner. Did you score big?"

"I could get a couple tanks of gas."

"Gosh, it must be nice to be considered a child."

"Actually, it wasn't a fun evening," Raina said. She told her friend about the miserable dinner with her family. "What if I jumped to the wrong conclusion about the money situation?" She swallowed the catch in her voice. "Do you think I did it deliberately to punish Po Po?"

"No. Don't even go there. You're both victims here. Don't let this secret tear the two of you apart. Focus on restitution and with time, your relationship with your grandma will repair itself."

"I don't even want to deal with investigating Martin's murder anymore. What's the point? My mother will not thank me."

"So you need her approval to get on with things now? Do you need her to wipe your bum and kiss your boo-boo, too?"

Raina chuckled. Yeah, tough love was exactly what she needed at the moment. "Thank you. I'll see you by the end of the week."

"Oh, good. I can't wait to introduce you to my new man. He's a keeper," Eden said. Every guy had been a keeper according to her friend.

They said their goodbyes and hung up. Before she could return her phone to her pocket, it dinged, indicating a text message.

It was from Smith.

You got yourself a deal.

Raina fist pumped the air. Hot diggity dog. Finally some good news.

She flew into the guest bedroom—throwing on clothes with wild abandon. This was it. Her chance to redeem herself to her grandma. She thanked her ancestors and even whistled when she left the house.

The drive to the Japanese Tea Garden didn't take any longer than the last time, but it felt like forever with the bumper-to-bumper traffic across town and winding along Martin Luther King Jr Drive. Why couldn't Smith choose someplace less popular with the tourists? She didn't know what Smith's fascination was with the place, but the bared cherry and wisteria trees were depressing to look at in the damp and fog. Maybe she could ask him about it.

Her footsteps thudded on the wooden floor planks as she climbed Drum Bridge to where Smith waited for her at the highest point on the arch. She stood next to him, pulling up the collar of her jacket. He towered over her by a mere two inches. If she huffed and puffed at his blond hair she might deflate it enough so they would be the same height.

He continued to stare at the jostling fishes in the pond even though she knew he was aware of her presence. His tapered hands looked frail as they hung over the rails on the bridge. "I proposed to my fiancée on this bridge the day before she died."

Raina tucked her hands into her armpits and stiffened to keep the shivering from showing. This feud between Smith and Sonny ran deep. She didn't know whether to be worried for the detective or the triad leader. Or maybe it would be smarter to worry about herself. The sacrificial lamb between Titans always got pulverized in the battle.

"If you lie to me, I will crush you." His hands curled into fists. "I will reach into the little small town of yours and squeeze the life out of you even if I take an entire lifetime to do it."

A bolt of fear settled on her chest, but she managed to wheeze out, "Understood. The information is good. And for the record, I have no ties with the Nine Dragons."

He glanced up, studying her eyes. "Good. I would hate to take down a nice girl like you." He pulled out the journal from a pocket inside his jacket and held out his other hand.

Raina dug in her purse for the yellow crêpe paper Sonny had given her a few nights ago. She unfolded it so the Nine Dragons chop's red ink sparkled in the light. "Just like in the olden days. The stamp is from a Chinese chop, probably carved into a block of jade or obsidian. I wonder if only the Dai Lo has this chop or if the other levels of the organization—"

"No wonder you're an academic. Do you know how many people died from one of these orders?"

Raina flushed at his assessment of her personality. He was right because she hadn't thought about all the people Sonny Kwan maimed or killed with one swift stamp of his chop. "I'm sorry," she stammered, "I blather when I'm scared."

"What are you afraid of?"

"I'm afraid my ignorance will get me killed."

His hatchet face tightened, but his lips curled into a mirthless smile. "I'm glad you have a brain in that head of yours."

They exchanged the journal and yellow paper. He studied the Chinese writing with an intense look on his face like he was trying to puzzle out the combination on a locked safe.

Raina shifted from foot to foot, unsure if she should take off with the book. When she couldn't bear it any longer, she blurted out, "Do you need me to translate it for you?"

"Eleven fifteen at the Port of Oakland."

Her eyebrows rose, but she shouldn't have been surprised. In his obsession, he would have learned the language so he could overhear information to take the triad down. "Okay, I'm going to leave now."

She strolled off the bridge with a casualness she didn't feel. At the foot, she glanced up the arch, but he had turned away from her. His shoulders shook, and he appeared shrunken. If he were anyone else, she would say he was crying.

She jogged the rest of the way back to her car. Inside the vehicle, she hit the locks and breathed deeply for the first time.

Raina clutched the journal in her hands. In less than twenty-four hours Sonny Kwan would come for this. She would need to move fast if she were to get the information she needed from this little book before it disappeared again. She pulled out her cell phone to text at the number Sonny had given her earlier.

HOOK, LINE, AND SINKER. GOOD LUCK.

Maybe a little devil whispered in her ear, but she added a second message.

YOU NEVER TOLD ME WHAT HAPPENED TO YOUR CLOTHES.

His cell phone would probably get thrown in the trash after receiving her text. She didn't know why she'd added the second message, but curiosity had made her do dumb things before.

Her phone dinged. The message was from Sonny.

I GOT BLOOD ON MINE. THE CLOTHES CAME FROM A LAUNDROMAT.

She shivered at the text. They were bound by their

grandfathers' shared history, but she hoped never to encounter Sonny Kwan again in this lifetime.

RAINA RACED through the traffic-clogged streets and made it back to the Victorian in record time— half an hour. She ran up the stairs and into her brother's bedroom to use his computer and scanner. She hadn't bothered to bring her laptop to San Francisco because she'd thought she would only stay for a few days when she'd packed.

The laptop and scanner powered on and she was in business. Each page took an eternity while the machine whirred and screeched. She didn't dare to slow down by reading the pages. There would be plenty of time to peruse the book after she was done. By her estimation, she had until tomorrow morning before Sonny Kwan would come to collect the journal.

Her cell phone rang, and she picked up. "Hello?"

"...Napa Valley Recovery Center...called...Rice..."

"You're breaking up." She glanced down at the network indicator on her phone. There were no bars. "I'll call you back on the house phone."

Raina ran downstairs and snatched the kitchen phone off its cradle. She wanted to make sure there would be no static when she heard what Brandi had to say about Hudson's finances. As she punched in the phone number for the rehab center, the front door clicked open. She was pressing the key combination to get a live person when Mom sailed into the kitchen, heading straight for the refrigerator.

The receptionist picked up the phone. "Napa Valley Recovery Center."

She gave her mom a sideways glance. Now what? She didn't want her mother to listen in on the conversation. "This is Raina Sun. You called me a few seconds ago."

"Sorry, we called several people. What is this regarding?"

"I asked the nurse to check in on a friend this morning."

"Who's the friend?"

"Um..."

The receptionist sighed. "Could you hold, please?" Elevator music came on.

"Is Eden all right?" Mom mouthed.

Raina gave her mother the okay sign with her hand, and Mom wandered out of the room and headed upstairs. This was close. Nothing worse than to hear bad news about your fiancé from eavesdropping on a conversation.

"Hello, ma'am? Are you still here?" said the voice in the phone line.

"Yes," Raina answered eagerly. "I called earlier about Brandi Rice. Did one of the nurses check on her?"

"How come you didn't say so earlier?" the receptionist said, a hint of irritation in her voice.

"Sorry. Her mother was in the room with me and I didn't want her to overhear our conversation. You know how mothers are. She's already worried enough as it is about Brandi." The lie rolled smoothly out of her mouth.

There was the sound of flipping pages. "Here it is. This is odd. She had a visitor early this morning, checked herself out, and left with him."

Mom came back down the stairs and poked her head into the kitchen. When she saw Raina was still on the phone, she tiptoed in and handed her a note. The front door slammed, and she was gone. Typical.

Raina tucked the paper into her jeans pocket. "What do you mean she checked out? Who was the visitor? Don't you have procedures to keep something like this from happening?"

"This is a recovery center, not a jail. Our patients are here voluntarily, and they can leave anytime."

She took a deep breath to steady her voice. This wasn't the receptionist's fault. "Brandi is hiding from an abusive boyfriend. She wants to end the relationship. She asked my family for help, and we thought the recovery center would be a safe haven since it's outside the City. Who was her visitor? Was he the boyfriend?"

"Let me call you back. I need to check the log book and talk to the director. I'm not supposed to give out confidential information about our patients." The receptionist hung up with a brisk click.

Raina slammed the phone back on the cradle. Her grandma was right—there was something satisfying in smacking the receiver down.

She couldn't believe Brandi Rice would walk away without contacting someone. Wasn't the recovery center supposed to be the safest place for her? Everyone knew drug addicts didn't always make the best decisions. What if her deadbeat boyfriend was the one who came to get her?

She shoved her hands into her pockets in frustration. Her fingers curled around the note Mom had given her.

She pulled it out and opened it. Her heart stopped beating. This had to be a mistake.

Taking journal to Martin's for séance to find his killer.

With shaking hands, Raina grabbed the kitchen phone again and dialed her mother's cell phone number. "Pick up, Mom. Pick up."

The call went straight to voicemail. She cursed her luck and left a message for her mother to call her back. She called Hudson and got voicemail again. They must have had their phones off for the ceremony.

What kind of incompetent fool would have a séance on Chinese New Year? She couldn't believe her mother went along with the scheme. Geez, no wonder business for his feng shui consultation was down the toilet. If Raina didn't stop them, her mom would deal with spirits, and angry ones at that, during the Year of the Monkey.

To drive across town again, get the journal, and come back to the Victorian would take at least three hours, cutting into the time she had left before Sonny Kwan came for the journal. Why was her mother doing this to her?

The kitchen phone rang, and she snatched up the receiver. "Hello? Mom?"

"This is Tina, calling you back from the Napa Valley Recovery Center," said the receptionist.

"Did you find out who Brandi left with?" Raina asked.

"Yes, ma'am, it was her brother—Hudson Rice."

19

STORMING THE CASTLE

Raina thanked the receptionist and hung up. Did Hudson get his sister for the séance? The idiot probably thought it was all fine and dandy to bring the whole family together to contact Martin on the other side.

She still had no idea who killed Martin. Joley Mok had no motive and turned out to work for Martin. And Sonny Kwan didn't seem the type to not take credit for the hit. With these two suspects eliminated, this left one of the Rice siblings, but which one? Martin was worth more to them when he was alive than dead. Hudson needed his help to keep the family business going, and Brandi could have gotten back into his good graces with time. It made no sense. And her mother was in the middle of it all.

Tangling with murderers wasn't something she took lightly. She could call Smith if she had an ounce of proof, which she didn't other than her hunch. How could she explain that her Chinese intuition was zinging like a metal detector over rusted soda cans? He was probably busy setting up for the sting operation to capture Sonny this evening.

Raina slammed a fist on the counter and winced at the pain. Geez, why did she always have to save her mom? She should drive back to Gold Springs and the safe cocoon she'd built for herself there. Her mom was a grown woman who could take care of herself—and pigs flew to the moon.

There was only one person who could help her now. She called Po Po and got her voicemail. As she headed out the door, she left her grandma a detailed message about her rescue mission at Martin's townhouse. If nothing else, her grandma could "pick up the bones" as the Chinese saying went, if things ended badly.

When Raina got to the Richmond District, she found a parking spot around the corner from the townhouse. With luck, she could approach the home undetected from the smaller street. Maybe she could even sneak in from the window on the side yard which she'd failed to do with Po Po the first time. That was as far as she got with her planning. And if Brandi had a gun, then any pre-planning on Raina's part would be for naught anyway.

The street was busy as usual, but everyone kept their heads down and trotted with a purpose that meant they wouldn't care if someone screamed bloody murder. The rolling fog and chill weren't conducive to loitering and small talk. She was half hoping to find Gigi yapping like she normally did, but no dice.

Raina let herself into the side yard. The gate swung

open as if the hinges had recently been oiled, which was odd since the little paved pad looked much as it did before—trash and recycle bins against the fence and smeared tomatoes in front of it. Martin never got the chance to clean up the mess Raina and Po Po made the last time they were here. Did the murderer come in through this way to kill Martin?

She wheeled the trash bin underneath the window, the plastic wheel rumbling on the pavers like someone who gorged too much on a Thanksgiving feast. Taking a deep breath, she climbed up on the flimsy plastic container and reached for the window. It slid up with a groan. She held her breath but continued to push the window open, one inch at a time. City dwellers were trained to ignore road noise and background sounds with such close living quarters. And both Hudson and Brandi had lived in the City their entire life.

Raina stuck her head into the opening. The narrow hallway was dark and empty. Good. She threw a leg across the sill and climbed in. The drapes were drawn over the windows for the séance. She hoped no one noticed the pale light that followed her entrance.

She crept to the guest bathroom and bedroom to make sure there weren't any surprises in them. They looked just like any other spare rooms. An old bed and storage boxes. Now what? She had a Monkey Fist, a package of firecrackers, and lighter. Not exactly weapons of mass destruction or even enough to put the fear of G—

Footsteps shuffled in the hallway.

Raina took a step backward until her legs bumped against the bed. She dropped to the ground and rolled underneath it, stirring up decades of dust on the shag carpeting. She held her breath. *Don't come in.*

"What are you planning to do with her?" Brandi spat, like a wet angry cat.

"Nothing. We're going to 'accidentally' burn the journal and hopefully that would be the end of all talk about Uncle Martin's cannibalism," Hudson said.

Raina slid her cell phone out of her pocket and tapped on the recorder app. Did the two of them conspire to kill Martin Eng for his shameful secret?

"What was that?" Brandi asked.

"What was what?"

Shoes appeared in the gap between the floor and the bottom of the bed.

"I thought I saw some kind of light in the room," Brandi said.

Raina held her breath. The cell phone display light!

"Don't be such a chicken butt. It's not even a real séance," Hudson said.

"And hence, why the family business is in trouble in the first place."

"What is that supposed to mean? Are you saying I'm a fraud?" He sounded indignant. "It's not my fault Uncle Martin's secret would have ruined the business. What was the man thinking to take up cannibalism again after all these years?"

"Are you sure no one else knows about this? And this is the only evidence? I swear, Hudson—"

"What's taking so long?" Mom called from the hallway.

Heeled boots, which had to be Brandi's, crossed the room. The closet door slid open. "Here's the joss paper."

"Come on, honey. Let's get this show on the road. We'll give Uncle Martin a proper sending off so his spirit can stop lingering..." Hudson's voice faded as they went back into the living room.

Raina lay there stunned, staring at the box spring and breathing in the dusty air. She turned off the recorder app and put the phone in the zipper pocket of her jacket for safekeeping. It had never crossed her mind there would be two murderers.

Especially since they both had alibis. Hudson was with her mom. She'd walked in on them in the dining room that morning. How would her mother take the news her fiancé was a murderer? And Brandi was in a domestic abuse situation with flashing cop lights and all. How could she make it to Martin's townhouse after such a beating?

If Raina left now, pretending like she hadn't recorded anything, and collected her mom at the front door, would the Rice siblings let the two of them go? But then she would lose the journal since the Rice siblings planned to burn it as a sacrifice to their uncle.

And she needed the journal if she was to make amends with her grandma. Without the secrets contained between its covers, her family might never find out why their former patriarch had another family waiting in the wings.

She wiggled on her stomach to get out from underneath the bed. The phone dug painfully in her side, but she couldn't move the phone without pinning her arm in the tight space. Fabulous. She got her torso out when the notes of "Fight Song" filled the air followed by a vibration that sent a stab of fear straight from her mid-section to her heart.

She scrambled out and fumbled with the zipper on her pocket. The phone continued to buzz and sing. She turned it off. The call was from Cassie. As usual, her sister had a great sense of timing.

A shadow fell across the threshold. Raina glanced up to see Brandi tapping a baseball bat on her palm. Great. She gave the woman a weak smile. "I'm ready to have a chat with Uncle Martin."

"Nice try. I knew there was something fishy when I saw that flash of light." Brandi pointed to a spot in front of her. "Put your phone right there."

Raina tossed the phone on the floor. No way was she arguing. She took a step back to put more space between them. Good thing all her data was backed up on the cloud.

Brandi swung the bat, smashing the cell phone until pieces scattered across the floor.

"Hey! Po Po gave me the phone for Christmas," Raina said.

"Oops. The bat slipped. Don't try any funny business or it'll be your head next."

Raina wrinkled her brow in pretend confusion. "What's the big deal? My mother invited me to a séance. The front door was locked, and I didn't want to interrupt the ceremony."

"Drop the act. You heard the conversation between Hudson and me. Now march. I want you in the living room with your mother." Brandi stepped aside so Raina could pass her.

"Did you kill your uncle or was it your brother?

Hudson has everything to gain from Martin's death," Raina said, rooted to the ground.

"Move it."

"Someone has to take the fall for Martin's murder. With forensics these days, your DNA is all over the pillow and under Martin's fingernails."

Raina had no idea if this were true, but with television exaggerating every criminal investigation, she thought it sounded like the real deal. All she needed was to plant the seed of doubt.

Brandi shifted her eyes away from Raina. "Hudson will help get me out of the state and give me some money to start a new life somewhere else."

"You'll be a fugitive while he gets to reap all the rewards here." Raina paused, watching doubt and anger cross Brandi's face. "So how did he talk you into it?"

"He would help me leave my boyfriend," Brandi whispered. "I had no choice."

"But Po Po could have helped you. All you had to do was ask."

Brandi shook her head, a tear slipping out of her eye. "Hudson is family."

"What's taking so long?" Hudson called from the living room.

Brandi jumped, dropping the baseball bat. It rolled across the carpet and touched Raina's shoe. It took all her willpower to not grab the bat and knock Brandi out with it. If Raina made a big ruckus now, Hudson would come roaring in and she wasn't physically strong enough to take on the two of them. Her best bet would be to divide and conquer the Rice siblings by creating doubt and confusion.

"Move it," Brandi said.

"This is just another form of abuse. He's using you to do his dirty work."

Brandi's jaw tightened, but she pointed at the hallway with the bat. "Have you ever seen what a bat could do to a watermelon?"

20

PERFUME DE RAINA

Raina's shoulder blades itched during the short walk from the guest room to the living room. She didn't like having Brandi behind her, smacking the bat against her palm. She knew very well what a busted watermelon looked like.

Her mother glanced up in surprise from the sofa when Raina entered the room. She held the journal in her hands.

Hudson's eyes shifted from Raina to Brandi and then his face changed. It was almost like watching a ghost possess his body. The open curious expression was replaced by narrowed eyes, pinched lips, and shadows. It sent a chill down Raina's spine. Any hope of help from that direction would be in vain.

"What are you doing here, honey?" Mom asked. "How did you get in?"

Brandi shoved Raina until she fell onto her mother. Mom dropped Ah Gong's journal to catch Raina.

"Hey!" Mom protested. "What's wrong with you?" She glanced at Hudson. "What's going on here?"

Brandi pointed at Raina's purse. "Empty it on the coffee table."

Mom slipped the journal into her purse and stood, pulling Raina up with her. "I don't know what's going on here, but we're leaving. You can't have a séance with such negative energy in the room."

"No," Hudson said. "The two of you are not leaving this townhouse. Raina, empty your purse."

"Hudson—"

"I said empty your purse," Brandi yelled, smashing the bat onto the coffee table, leaving a dent on the wood.

Mom jumped as if prodded with a hot iron. Raina dumped the contents of her purse onto the floor. No gun or knife came tumbling out.

Brandi and Hudson relaxed as if expecting Raina would carry a weapon of mass destruction around in her purse like she would a tube of lip balm.

"You used my mom to give you an alibi on the night Martin died," Raina stated. "And now you'll let your sister take the fall even though the murder was your idea in the first place." It was a wild guess, but she was probably in the ballpark.

Brandi slid a sideways glance at Hudson as if waiting for his denial.

A dog outside yapped like an over-sensitive car alarm.

"I swear if that Mrs. Keane—"

A scratching started at the front door, growing more frantic. Raina held her breath. Come on, Gigi.

Brandi whispered, "What are we going to do now?"

"Everyone, stay quiet," Hudson said, his eyes on Mom and Raina. "Move a muscle and the other one dies."

Mom gasped, the implication finally sinking in. Her face was painful to watch—going from white to red in the blink of the eye. Hurt, fear, humiliation, and anger flashed across her face. Her knuckles whitened around the straps of her purse.

Raina's chest tightened and a flash of anger rose inside. No one got to treat her mom this way. She wanted to whack his head with the Monkey Fist her grandma had given her.

Brandi kept an eye on her mother, probably knowing a woman scorned could be more dangerous than any weapon.

Knock! Knock!

No one moved a muscle, but their eyes were all watching each other. Raina could feel her mother trembling next to her, poised for action.

The mail slot on the door lifted, and a patch of sunlight fell across the entryway. "Raina Sun, I know you're in there. I'm calling the police to let them know you broke into Martin Eng's house," Mrs. Keane called out, her voice ringing across the living room. "And I'm coming back with the spare key."

Gigi continued to bark, and the noise echoed deafeningly around the room. Mrs. Keane called out to her dog, but Gigi ignored her. There was a shuffling noise as if Mrs. Keane had to tug or drag the Boston terrier away. Apparently, perfume de Raina Sun was just too much for the little gal. As the barking faded from the front door, a collective sigh came from the Rice siblings.

A spark of hope settled on Raina's chest. All she had

to do was delay things until the police came. Easy peasy. "You should leave before the neighbor comes back."

"Shut up!" Hudson said.

"We can't leave them here. They'll tell the police everything," Brandi said.

He glowered at them, probably knowing the Sun women weren't meek sheep. "Then what do you suggest—batter them until they're a bloody mess? We don't exactly have the time for this."

"What do we do—"

A crash in the hallway cut Brandi off. What appeared to be smoke trickled into the room, mushrooming in size until it filled the living room in a pale haze. The dancing lava lamp was the only bright beacon in the mist.

"A fire!" Brandi dropped the bat and wrung her hands. "Uncle Martin is getting back at me. It wasn't my fault. It was Hudson's idea. He said he'd split the money from the house with me."

Hudson jerked his head toward the hall and pulled his shirt over his face. "There's no ghost in this house." His voice was muffled in his shirt.

Raina glanced at the green light on the fire alarm above Hudson's head. The green light was on, and it was quiet as a rock. Idiots. If she had to guess, her grandma was outside playing with her dry ice. She lit the package of firecrackers and threw it behind the sofa to add to the confusion.

Pop! Pop! Pop!

Mom dropped to the ground, covering her head with her hands. "Martin, are you here? Speak to us." Her eyes glinted as if she had rehearsed her lines.

Brandi moaned and pointed at the front door.

Hudson's gaze followed her finger. Something hurled against the door.

Bump! Bump! Bump!

Raina grabbed her keys and hurled it at Brandi. The monkey fist connected with her temple, her eyes rolled up, and she fell with a thump that would have made a fallen oak proud.

Hudson's eyes became hot and bright, and he dropped into a crouch. Moisture beaded on his upper lip, and his face became the color and texture of old paper. Either he believed Martin's spirit was in the room or he knew the jig was doing a handstand.

The front door crashed open and little Gigi bounced in, tail stiffening like an antenna and teeth flashing like a piranha. She circled in front of Hudson with high prancing steps as if led by a ghostly hand. Mrs. Keane screamed at the Boston terrier but didn't come in.

"It's a message from Martin," Mom called out from her huddle.

"I had to save the family business," Hudson muttered. "Your secret would have ruined us." His eyes continued to flit around the room as if searching for someone.

Another crash and Po Po and Cassie flew in from the hallway; both wore pink camo bandanas tied around their faces.

Hudson's head swiveled from the front door to the hall, his bulging eyes like a frozen doll.

Raina grabbed Mom and tossed her on the other side of the sofa. She leapt after her. "Against the walls," she yelled to her grandma and sister. The shag carpeting would have prevented the glass from breaking.

"What—"

"Just do it."

Ping! Ping! Ping!

Little glass vials shattered on the wood paneling, leaving wet trails where they made contact. If they were in a comic strip, the air would have poofed around them in a pea green cloud. As it was, there was a heartbeat of silence and then skunk funk filled the air, followed by rotting kimchi and the hot burn of chili pepper.

Raina closed her eyes, but tears streamed down her face unheeded. She swallowed the bile in the back of her throat, having been through this routine before. Breathing through her mouth didn't help.

Mom gagged next to her, clutching at her throat. The entire scene would have been comedic if it weren't so serious.

Po Po and Cassie came around the sofa. Her grandma grabbed Raina's arm, hauling her up, and Cassie did the same with their mom. By the time the four of them hustled out of the townhouse and onto the sidewalk, the faint wail of a police cruiser could be heard.

Mrs. Keane stood on her stoop, waving at the cops with a red-and-white-checkered kitchen towel like a used up pin-up doll for a street race. A crowd had gathered on the sidewalk, but no one made any attempt to go in. The dry ice continued to billow out the front door.

Hudson appeared in the doorway with wild red eyes and coughing up a storm. He tried to slink away in the crowd, but a big burly man grabbed his arm. Hudson twisted, trying to loosen the grip, and the burly man put him in a headlock.

A man in a gray hoodie walked away from the scene as the cops got out of their vehicles. Raina could have sworn the man had a scar on his face. Did Sonny Kwan follow her from the Victorian? Would he have helped if Po Po and her sister didn't show up? After all, compared to the Dai Lo of the Nine Dragon triad, Hudson and Brandi were just amateurs.

AFTER HOURS of answering police questions and a celebratory dinner, Cassie left for Daly City from the restaurant. The ride home was subdued as the adrenaline leaked out of them with each passing street sign. It was seven thirty when Raina pulled into the garage. Mom's car had been left at the crime scene. Po Po went upstairs with Mom.

Raina wanted nothing more than a good cry herself, like her mom undoubtedly was doing with Po Po rubbing her back. But she still had work to do and only a few hours left to do it. She crept into the hall closet and opened her mom's purse. Tucking the journal under her arm, she headed for her brother's room. The scanner was still on the desk, but his laptop was gone.

As her eyes inspected the room, her chest felt heavy like she was out of breath. Nothing was out of place. The tennis racket was still leaning against the bed. The drawers were still closed. No burglar or Nine Dragons goon.

She ran downstairs to grab her mom's cell phone and texted her brother.

THIS IS RAINA. DID YOU COME BACK FOR YOUR LAPTOP? I NEED TO USE IT.

He replied instantly.

Yep, working on an essay for school.

Raina ground her teeth in frustration. Of all the times for her to be without her laptop. She needed a computer to finish up the scanning.

Did you touch the files on the desktop? When are you going to be home?

She reminded herself to breathe. There was still time for her to scan the rest of the journal. The cell phone dinged.

I thought they were Mom's. Sorry, deleted them. Around eight thirty.

Her heart sank. All the scanning in the morning for nothing. She swallowed her panic. Okay, it would be an all-nighter, but she could still do it. She would wait for Win to get home. It would take her longer to drive over to Daly City to use Cassie's computer.

She went to the spare bedroom and flopped down on the floral bedspread, cradling the journal in her arms. She could hear muffled crying in another room, and her heart ached for her mom, but she knew her presence wouldn't be welcomed.

The warm room and full belly after an afternoon like this one lulled her senses until her limbs grew heavy. She programmed the alarm clock on the nightstand to wake her in an hour and closed her eyes to chase after the Sandman.

Beep! Beep! Beep!

Raina opened her eyes to a dark room. Someone turned off the lights. She yawned, glancing at the digital display on the alarm clock. Eight-thirty. Her brother should be home with his laptop any minute now. She staggered to the light switch and clicked it on. As the light flooded the room, she blinked at the quick transition from darkness to light.

Lying on the chair at the foot of the bed was the purple cashmere scarf she'd loaned Sonny Kwan on the day they met. Gooseflesh peppered her arms and she stiffened to keep from shivering. She glanced around the room but knew it was a futile act.

He would be long gone by now. And apparently, he felt they were on friendly enough terms for him to pick up her grandfather's journal while she napped. He'd played her for a fool.

She doubted there was any kind of shipment coming in later this evening. Smith wouldn't be her BFF after he found out she'd given him false information on the Nine Dragons.

Now how was she to get the journal back from the clutches of the Nine Dragons? Offer herself as the sacrificial lamb? She snorted. This only worked if someone actually wanted her.

21

A NEW RAIN

The next day Raina met with her grandfather's lawyer and then left San Francisco. She didn't have time to have a heart-to-heart chat with her mom, but she wasn't worried. Po Po had stayed behind to keep an eye on things. While her mom might have cared for Hudson, Raina suspected most of the tears came from wounded pride rather than a broken heart. She wished she was the type to boo-hoo with her mother, but she didn't have the patience for it.

The next week in Gold Springs was a quiet one. She stayed busy catching up with schoolwork and looking for another part-time job. Her boss had opted to hire the fellow graduate student Raina had called to fill-in for her while she was in the Bay Area. Detective work wasn't without personal sacrifices.

Raina just came through the front door from another interview when someone knocked. She tossed her purse on the side table and automatically glanced at the spot above the television where she'd hung a gilded koi clock once upon a time. She opened the door to find Cassie on the other side. "What are you doing here? Where's Lila?"

"You really opened a can of worms," said her older sister, pushing her way into the apartment. She nodded at the pile of socks next to her stack of books at the base of the sofa. "I see you still have your little hoarder tendencies."

Raina shifted from foot to foot. She wasn't a hoarder; she was a piler. What could be made into a molehill or a stack became one in her home. But correcting her sister wasn't worth the effort, not with someone who ran on the façade of perfection. It must be pretty draining to be so neat.

"Do you want to sit down?" She gestured at the new-to-me sofa underneath her living room window. "Thank you, by the way, for the sofa. It's perfect." Yes, there was the word again.

"No, I need to stretch my legs after the drive. I can see why you like this little town. The historic downtown area is charming," Cassie said.

Raina sprawled on the sofa while her sister paced the small living room. Even though she lived in Gold Springs for over a year, it was the first visit from her sister. Should she offer Cassie a drink? "Are you an ambassador for our family?"

"Kind of. Uncle Anthony is all charged up to find his half-brother. He wants to hire Matthew for the job."

Raina frowned at the thought of her ex-boyfriend doing side jobs for her eldest uncle. When would their lives stop intersecting? "How's Po Po taking everything?"

"She is still upset with you, for the way you broke the news—which I think is awesome." A mischievous smile crossed her sister's face along with the dimple on the side of her chin and then disappeared like she didn't want to encourage Raina's bad behavior. "I think she had it in her head it was all a mistake, and there was no secret family. You burst her little delusion."

Raina ignored the self-importance in her sister's voice. "Do you know when she will come back to Gold Springs?"

"I think she might put her condo on the market. I'm here to gather some of her stuff."

If Raina had to guess, she would say Po Po was staying in the City to monitor what Uncle Anthony might dig up. Until the ink dried on the contract, she wouldn't take her sister's assessment too seriously. "I see."

"You know how she is—she gets an idea and jumps before she thinks it through. She could always buy another unit if the sale is a mistake."

But the new unit wouldn't be right next door to her best friend. "This must be a relief for you. Now you don't have to worry about Po Po selling the house from underneath Mom."

"You don't have to get nasty about it. I'm just the messenger."

"Sorry. I mean it. At least we don't have to worry about Mom being homeless. How is she doing?"

Cassie shook her head. "Well enough after Po Po talked her out of shaving her hair to become a Buddhist nun."

Raina felt guilty for revealing Hudson as Martin's killer, but her mom had insisted she get involved. "I guess this reaction was better than the numbness she felt when dad died."

Cassie shrugged, dismissing their mother's grief. She probably didn't want to remember how she fell apart after their father's death either. "Uncle Anthony decided to split the first million dollars between all of us cousins. Each of us gets fifty-thousand dollars. He'll pay for the rest of your grad school tuition so you won't have to use your inheritance on your education." Her sister gave her a crooked smile. "I guess you must find yourself a real job."

Raina ignored the bait. Fifty-thousand dollars and back in her family's good graces? She must have hit the karma jackpot...except it felt like she got voted off the island. "What will happen to the rest of the two million dollars? Is Uncle Anthony sending it to his half-brother?"

"I don't know. It depends on what Matthew digs up."

"And you're happy with this decision?"

"Anything is better than one dollar."

Raina nodded, not so much in agreement, but as a ploy to get rid of her sister. "I'm glad everyone is happy with this decision."

"I don't understand why you think Ah Gong's secret was yours alone. It impacts our entire family—and guess what? No one appreciated the secrecy."

And hence the difference between the two of them. "I was trying to protect the family. I was afraid of the fallout."

Cassie shook her head as if Raina lost one too many brain cells. "We didn't need your protection. No one asked you to take on this role. You isolated yourself from the rest of the family for nothing."

Her sister was wrong. "You think the family would have been able to handle this news at the eve of Ah

Gong's death? And you expect me to tell our dying grandfather 'no' at his bedside?"

"What's wrong with lying? It's not like he would know after he's gone. The family would have been able to deal with it. Instead we had this drama between you and the cousins—first a lawsuit and then picking sides. We kept ripping the scab off an old wound. You could have trusted me with Ah Gong's secret. I would have helped you."

Raina stared at her sister. No matter what she said, it would be misinterpreted. "You already have enough on your plate with a new baby. I didn't want to add to it." This was technically true.

Cassie studied her for a long moment. "I appreciate it because you're right—I wouldn't have been able to handle the truth." She gave a long sigh. "Being smack in the middle of our large family is hard with so many cousins and their running list of alphabets after their names. But this middle child's need to please everyone is only going to break your heart someday. You got to learn to say no, kiddo."

Raina stiffened. Middle child syndrome? Oh please! At least she wasn't walking around pretending everything was perfect when things were falling through the cracks at home. And did Uncle Anthony expect her to sit back and let Matthew finish the investigation on her family? Fat chance. Unlike her ex-boyfriend, she still had an ace in the hole.

"Well, at least someone appreciates it," Raina said, not bothering to disguise the peevish tone creeping into her voice.

Cassie chuckled as if Raina was a child who said something amusing. "I better hit the road so I don't end up in rush hour traffic when I get to the Bay Area. Take care of yourself."

Raina shut the door after her sister and whipped out her cell phone. Po Po had been a prophet when she'd bought insurance on the cell phone she'd given Raina for Christmas. She lifted her head, staring at the blank space above her television.

Her Uncle Anthony stepped in as the patriarch of the family to investigate the secret family. He had also taken over the disbursement of the three million dollars. Wasn't this the best possible outcome? She could walk away. She could finally be free. No more holding on to a fortune for a half-uncle she'd never met. No more searching for a journal with the longevity symbol and tangling with the triad.

Her heart pounded, but she had no choice. Either she would let someone else dictate her life or she would take care of business herself. Her fingers flew across the screen on her phone.

You're a lying cheating rat who should be cursed the next time I step into a temple.

She held her breath, waiting for a response. She was gambling that her instinct had been correct. For all she knew, Sonny Kwan could send one of his goons to chop off her head with the mere flicker of his pinkie finger.

The cell phone chirped. Her hands trembled as she tapped on the message icon.

Then come spank me.

The cell phone chirped again. It was an address in Canada.

The breath rushed out of her. She had been right. If she wasn't meant for this job, her ancestors wouldn't have assigned it to her. Who was a mere mortal like her dictatorial uncle to interfere with things he didn't understand?

An overwhelming sense of victory came over her. Raina fist pumped and pranced around the room. She went into the kitchen to dig in the freezer. This new beginning needed her best buds—Ben and Jerry—to help her celebrate.

THE END

PLEASE REVIEW my books at your *ebook retailer*. As an indie author, reviews help other readers find my books. I appreciate all reviews, whether positive or negative.

Continue Raina's story now.
Balmy Darlings and Death (Raina Sun #4)

ALSO BY ANNE R. TAN

Thanks for reading *Breezy Friends and Bodies*. I hope you enjoyed it!

Did you like this book?

Please review my books at your *ebook retailer*. As an indie author, reviews help other readers find my books. I appreciate all reviews, whether positive or negative.

Want to know about new releases, sale pricing, and exclusive content?

Sign up for Anne R. Tan's email newsletter at http://annertan.com/newsletter

Your information would not be sold or transferred. Thank you for trusting me with your email.

Want More Raina Sun?

Raining Men and Corpses (Raina Sun #1)

Gusty Lovers and Cadavers (Raina Sun #2)

Breezy Friends and Bodies (Raina Sun #3)

Balmy Darlings and Death (Raina Sun #4)

Sunny Mates and Murders (Raina Sun #5)

Murky Passions and Scandals (Raina Sun #6)

Smoldering Flames and Secrets (Raina Sun #7)

Hazy Grooms and Homicides (Raina Sun #8)

Chilly Comforts and Disasters (Raina Sun #9)

How about another series by Anne R. Tan?

Just Shoot Me Dead (Lucy Fong #1)

Just Lost and Found (Lucy Fong #1.5)

Just a Lucy Break-In (Lucy Fong #2)

BALMY DARLINGS AND DEATHS

Raina tugged up the strap of her push-up bra—part of a fancy set she'd gotten from her grandma for her birthday —to keep from snapping her fingers at the man's face so he could stay with her in the conversation. It would be rude, but the receptionist at the day spa kept returning to the same point—her gift certificate wasn't in their system.

She'd been here for thirty minutes trying to make an appointment. If this their customer service, did she need a fancy hairdo this badly? But if she rejected this gift certificate, her best friend Eden might interpret it as a rejection of her. Her friend probably went without gas in her car for a week to gift Raina this treat.

It didn't help Raina was getting a neck cramp from looking at the tall young man in black skinny jeans, and a fitted sateen shirt. His smooth olive skin and the lock of brown hair across his forehead gave him an exotic foreign air, except she didn't like his bleary eyes and the loopy smile on his face. He had to be on medication.

"I don't know what to say, ma'am." He held the slip of

paper up against the light as if checking for counterfeit money. "Where did you get the gift certificate? Are you sure your friend bought it from us?"

He meant the exclusive Inner Beauty Day Spa, known for creating miracles among the women who bypassed the make-up and hair experimentation stage in their teens and twenties.

The small front area was meant to be Zen-like with its minimalist decor and the natural light coming from the glass front windows, but it reminded Raina of a down on its luck rental office. There was one loveseat, a potted plant, and the receptionist counter. The rest of the day spa was hidden behind a beaded curtain.

Raina pointed at the embossed logo on the card stock paper. "Are you having problems keeping your gift certificates off the black market? I'm not trying to wrangle a free haircut."

The receptionist glanced at the ceiling as if praying this was a bad dream. "I'm not sure we have anyone who can handle...your hair."

Patience grasshopper, said a small voice in her head.

Raina tucked a curl behind her ear. She wasn't leaving without her miracle. "How is my Chinese hair any different than your brown hair?"

"I meant the perm."

She laughed and pointed at her head. "Do you think I would pay for this rat's nest? It's natural. Why do you think I'm here? I need a miracle."

Geez, did the man not know anything about genetics? It was bad enough sometimes her own cousins made fun of her curly hair, but the recessive gene ran in both sides of her family. Of her parent's children, Raina won the genetic lottery. Yippee. Chinese girl with a dandelion hair.

The bell on the glass door behind her chimed. Raina glanced behind her to see two ladies settling on the loveseat and chuckling into their hands. Heat rose to Raina's face. They could be laughing at a joke among themselves. The beaded curtain parted, a clinking sound, and Raina spun around to see her best friend Eden Small, stepping into the room.

"Eden, please explain to this gentleman"—Raina's voice dripped with sarcasm at the last word—"that I didn't steal this gift certificate."

Her best friend glanced at the receptionist. "Walt, could I speak to you for a minute." She dragged him to a corner.

Raina couldn't make out the whispered conversation, but by the frown on Walt's face and the pleading look on Eden's, it wasn't good. *So much for a sleek birthday hairdo.* She checked the time on her cell phone.

This was customer service at its finest. Good thing her last final was tomorrow, or she would have to come up with money to retake the history graduate class again.

She glanced at the two ladies behind her. They weren't even trying to hide their interest in the whispered conversation. While Raina might be a passing interest, Eden was the Assistant Chief-in-Editor for the town's weekly newspaper, which meant the town watched her BFF with a mixture of curiosity and fear for the buzz she generated when chasing a lead.

Walt returned to the receptionist counter and tapped on the monitor screen to bring up a calendar. Eden gave Raina a thumb up sign before disappearing behind the beaded curtain. The waiting ladies whispered to each other, their voices like singing magpies. If they only knew her friend worked part-time stocking the treatment rooms and doing general cleanup it would embarrass her friend.

"We're not supposed to use the employee discount for gift certificates. Happy birthday," Walt said to the monitor.

Raina bet her lucky underwear he didn't treat paying customers this way. He was lucky they weren't in a dark alley together or she would stuff one of her grandma's ultra strong stink bombs in his mouth and pulled his underwear over his head. *Super wedgie anyone?*

The bell above the front door chimed again. Walt glanced up with a smile, but it slipped when he recognized the muscular brunette. She was taller than most men, and her three-inch stilettos emphasized this. Her skin was a shade of bronze that women paid handsomely to fake from a bottle, but was probably the result of her mixed race.

Raina stared openly at the beauty. Of course, the Amazonian beauty had high cheekbones and big eyes. Nope, Raina wasn't the least bit bitter at the DNA roulette.

"Where is the home-wrecker?" the brunette asked, hands on her hips, her gaze sweeping through the small front area as if expecting this person to jump out from behind the loveseat.

"Hello to you too, LaShawna," Walt said. "Do you want to make an appointment?" His tone was polite enough, but there was an edge to it. He pointedly ignored her question.

Raina's eyes widened in recognition. LaShawna Robertson was the ex of Eden's new boyfriend. Nothing good would come from a confrontation between the two, especially in a gossip hotspot like the day spa.

"Where is the home-wrecker? Where is Eden Small?" LaShawna demanded again.

Raina stepped closer to the beaded curtain, waiting for an opportunity to slip inside to warn her friend. Her friend was no homewrecker, but this false accusation would travel around the small town of Gold Springs faster than the spread of an STD.

The room went silent. Everyone appeared to be holding their breath.

"Who are you talking about?" Walt finally asked.

LaShawna leaned in to speak, but Raina slipped through the beaded curtain without waiting to hear the words. The dimly lit lounge area with lilting soft music and a spritz of sugarly scent was meant to encourage intimate conversation or mediation. There were overhead spot lamps the customers could turn on for reading while they waited.

The wide arched entryway on her left opened to the salon chairs for hair and make-up. The rice paper screens for the four treatment rooms were closed. She found her friend wheeling a cart with fluffy white towels and a tray of seaweed toward the rice paper screened treatment rooms.

"Eden!" Raina whispered.

Her friend glanced up. Heavy footsteps thudded behind Raina, and she saw her friend's eyes widened in surprise. A large hand slammed into Raina's back, shoving her against the wall, and a large body hurled herself toward Eden.

"Home-wrecker!" LaShawna screeched.

Raina straightened, wincing at what would no doubt be a bruise on her back. The adult thing would be to calm LaShawna down, even if it meant swallowing Raina's rising anger at being manhandled. While genetics unfortunately made her the size of a pygmy goat, it didn't mean she should take being shoved with a smile.

Eden tipped her chin at LaShawna and opened her mouth, but LaShawna swung her open palm.

Crack!

Eden's head jerked back, her cheek reddened with a hand print. She stumbled into the cart and knocked over the stack of clean towels. LaShawna lunged forward, twisted Eden into a headlock, and tugged handfuls of the weave off her friend's head. Eden screamed and batted at the muscular arms holding her hostage. Their feet trampled on the white towels.

Raina hurled into LaShawna, using her shoulder like a battering ram, but her five-foot-three frame only bounced off the broad back. Her gaze scanned the hall for a weapon. Unless she could set fire to the rice paper screens, there wasn't much here to help her. So she did the next best thing and opened her mouth to scream.

LaShawna spun around and crammed a slick piece of seaweed into her mouth. Raina gagged at the moldy mushroom odor and salty briny taste. She tried to spit out the seaweed, but the larger woman's back pinned her against the wall. LaShawna half turned to grab for Eden again, bringing her sweaty unshaven armpits an inch from Raina's nose. She would die from suffocation.

Hands pulled LaShawna off. She struggled against several restraining hands. Eden sagged against the opposite wall with a bald patch on the right side of her head.

Raina spat out the glob of seaweed, and it landed on polished pink pumps. She gulped air like it was going out of style. She grimaced as she wiped LaShawna's sweat off her cheek.

"What's going on here?" Myra Jo asked, stepping between the woman and Eden. The spa owner looked like a miniature doll refereeing among heavyweight boxers. She looked from one woman to another, ignoring the seaweed on her pink pumps.

Women slipped out from their rice paper screen rooms to peek at the noise. They were in various stages of their treatment, their faces covered with black green and orange facial masks and wearing fluffy white bathrobes.

"Your employee attacked me." LaShawna tugged her half exposed bosom back into her strappy tank top. "She's jealous I'm have a child with her man."

Eden gingerly patted at her weave. "You're a no good lying rat. I was minding my own business when you grabbed me from behind."

Someone snickered from the crowd. Myra Jo tilted her head at the staff, and they corralled the women back into their treatment rooms. It took a few more minutes to sort things out with LaShawna. She threatened to sue the spa on the top of her lungs until Myra Jo threw in free mud treatments and hair coloring.

"For a year?" LaShawna asked, her eyes gleaming with greed.

"A week," Myra Jo said.

LaShawna crossed her arms. "A month."

"Fine." Myra Jo nodded at a woman wearing a polo shirt with the spa logo. "Please get LaShawna settled into one of the treatment rooms." She turned and stalked into an opposite corridor, expecting Eden to follow in her wake.

Eden hung her head and trudged after her boss, but not before Raina saw the pinched face and suppressed tears. Her friend needed this part-time gig like a fish needed water. The struggling weekly newspaper paid her in IOUs when businesses didn't fill the advertising spots. And it looked like Eden might have to join Raina in the unemployment line after this conversation with Myra Jo.

They continued to the opposite arched entryway, and it led to a narrow hallway with doors leading to the restrooms, the office, the walk-in storage closet, the staff break room, and the emergency exit. The dim sconces barely lit the hallway, but maybe it was meant to discourage the customers from wandering over to this part of the day spa.

As she crossed the threshold into the closet called an office, Raina felt like a child being sent to the principal's office. Myra Jo eased onto her chair, sighing as if she had been on her feet the entire morning. She gestured for them to sit.

Raina eyed the pile of paperwork teetering from the chair across from the battered desk. "I'll stand." She launched into the explanation of LaShawna barging in to the spa.

Eden studied her shoes during the entire recital. By the set of her hunched shoulders and clenched jaw, her pride and embarrassment at the pubic fight meant she wouldn't grovel for her job. But Raina knew pride didn't pay for the Frosted Flakes, her friend's breakfast of choice, nor the gas to get around town.

"Eden, even though you're my brother's girlfriend, I'll have to let you go. LaShawna has full custody of my nephew, and I can't antagonize her for my brother's sake," Myra Jo said, her face full of regret. "I'm sorry."

"Wait," Raina said. "It wasn't her fault. And Taylor and LaShawna aren't even together anymore. Why is she upset Eden is dating her ex?"

"It's okay, Raina." Eden nodded stiffly at Myra Jo. "I understand. I'll get my stuff."

"But Eden did nothing wrong," Raina said.

"It's fine," Eden said.

"No, it's not. It's not fair. You need this job," Raina said.

"I don't want trouble for my boyfriend's family," Eden whispered even though Myra Jo could hear everything she said.

The spa owner looked pensive, studying them through lowered eyes as if this would give them some privacy.

Raina wanted to rail at the injustice of the situation, but her friend wouldn't appreciate the interference. If only—

Boom!

The building shook, rattling the overhead light fixture. The pile of paperwork on the chair spilled onto the floor.

Raina's wide eyes studied the other two women. Was that a bomb?

Myra Jo, her face pinched and white, crouched in her seat. Eden's gazed scanned the room, looking for a threat.

The office door banged open and Walt stuck in his head. His eyes bright and alert. Something snapped him out of his reverie. "Myra Jo, a car ran into the side of the building. Connie is on the phone with the police."

Myra Jo stood, swaying slightly until she stiffened. "Oh, my God. Could this day get any worse?" She followed the receptionist outside with Eden hot on her heels.

Raina trotted after the two women, but lost track of them in the gathering crowd and unfamiliar building. Once again, women left their beauty treatments to check out the ruckus. If there was no special run on the *Gold Springs Weekly* tomorrow morning, then Eden was slacking off. Raina followed the herd outside and to the rear of the building. She squinted against the bright sunlight.

At the flash of red, Raina raced toward the crash scene with her heart in a vise. *Please don't let it be Po Po's car.* Her grandmother was still in San Francisco, but had left her car keys with her BFF in case the car had to be moved from the senior center parking lot.

A red Miata stuck out from the beauty salon side of the day spa, shattering three of the glass storefront windows. Part of the black-and-white-striped canopy covered the car like a shroud.

Join the fun. Buy now!
Balmy Darlings and Death
(Raina Sun #4)

ABOUT THE AUTHOR

Anne R. Tan fell in love with storytelling in elementary school, but decided to study engineering so she could get a "real job." Her day job is her vacation from home and she moonlights as a writer to keep the voices inside her head under control.

Her debut humorous cozy mysteries features Raina Sun, a Chinese American amateur sleuth, dealing with love, family betrayal, and her place in the world while solving murders.

If you are interested in learning more about Tan and her writing process, sign up for Anne R. Tan's email newsletter at http://annertan.com/newsletter for exclusive content, new release announcements, and sales.